Praise for *The Promise*

'A collection of 12 blistering stories.' *Good Reading*

'Throughout *The Promise* there's the sense of a writer who has landed in the sweet spot of his gift.'
The Weekend Australian

'Birch's fiction confronts the reader with rural and urban landscapes of abandonment, scenes of decay and decline. *The Promise* demands we go looking for that which is harder to see.' *Sydney Review of Books*

An 'impressive new collection.' *Books + Publishing*

'Tough, tight, powerful stories of love, loss and falling by the wayside from a master of the short-form genre.'
Qantas magazine

'Birch gives voice to characters often unheard.'
The Age

'Each story is very different but just as engaging. Birch has the ability to write interesting stories, often of everyday events, with vivid characters. An enjoyable read.'
The Big Book Club

Tony Birch is the author of three novels: the bestselling *The White Girl*, winner of the 2020 NSW Premier's Award for Indigenous Writing, and shortlisted for the 2020 Miles Franklin Literary Award; *Ghost River*, winner of the 2016 Victorian Premier's Literary Award for Indigenous Writing; and *Blood*, which was shortlisted for the Miles Franklin Literary Award. He is also the author of *Shadowboxing* and four short story collections: *Father's Day*, *The Promise*, *Common People* and *Dark as Last Night*. In 2017 he was awarded the Patrick White Literary Award for his contribution to Australian literature. Tony Birch is also an activist, historian and essayist. www.tony-birch.com

ALSO BY TONY BIRCH

Shadowboxing

Father's Day

Blood

Ghost River

Common People

Broken Teeth

The White Girl

Whisper Songs

Dark as Last Night

THE PROMISE

Tony Birch

UQP

First published 2014 by University of Queensland Press
PO Box 6042, St Lucia, Queensland 4067 Australia
Reprinted 2014, 2015, 2018, 2019, 2021, 2023

University of Queensland Press (UQP) acknowledges the Traditional Owners
and their custodianship of the lands on which UQP operates. We pay our respects
to their Ancestors and their descendants, who continue cultural and spiritual
connections to Country. We recognise their valuable contributions to Australian
and global society.

www.uqp.com.au
reception@uqp.com.au

© Tony Birch

Cover design and photograph by Josh Durham (Design by Committee)
Typeset in 12/16 pt Bembo by Post Pre-press Group, Brisbane
Printed in Australia by McPherson's Printing Group

National Library of Australia cataloguing-in-publication data is available
at http://catalogue.nla.gov.au

ISBN 978 0 7022 4999 0 (pbk)
ISBN 978 0 7022 5210 5 (epdf)
ISBN 978 0 7022 5211 2 (ePub)
ISBN 978 0 7022 5212 9 (Kindle)

University of Queensland Press uses papers that are natural, renewable
and recyclable products made from wood grown in well-managed forests
and other controlled sources. The logging and manufacturing processes
conform to the environmental regulations of the country of origin.

For Erin, Siobhan, Drew, Grace and Nina

CONTENTS

There will be no more mourning or crying or pain, for the old order of things has passed.
— REVELATION, 21:4

CHINA

I NEVER STOPPED LOVING CHINA. We got together in the summer we turned seventeen and spent warm nights under the pier drinking cider and smoking weed. Some nights we walked the back roads to the ocean and lay naked in the dunes looking up at the stars. One night China rolled her salty skin onto me, dropped warm tears on my shoulder and asked that we pray our love would last. I told her there was no need for prayers. As it was I didn't believe in any god, but swore we'd always be together.

I really did believe we'd make it, as long as I could stay out of trouble, which wouldn't be easy. I'd been fucking up since I started high school, and was forever deep in shit, with teachers and the local police.

When word got out that we were together, China's family and friends warned her off me. The town was small enough that we couldn't be together without word getting back to her father, a sheep farmer and champion trap shooter. He came after me like I was a bush dog that had crept up on and tore the throat out of one of his sheep in the night. We were forced to meet under the pier of a night and disappear into the shadows, where China would whisper that she loved me and trusted me and was ready to take a chance on me. For most of the year we were together I did stay out of trouble, not counting a fight here and there, which was no more than most local boys got up to on a drunken Saturday night.

China came to hate our hometown, the whispers and the gossip. She decided our future lay in escape. She took me by the hand down at the beach one night and told me that if I could land a job in the city she was ready to follow me. I didn't mind the town myself. I'd never been anywhere else and the idea of packing up for good didn't appeal to me.

'We could get jobs here, China.'

'Yeah, we could. A shit job for you. Maybe labouring on a farm. And the supermarket for me. I want more than that.' She let go of my hand. 'You can stay if you like, but I'm getting out of here by the end of the year.'

She walked off in her red bikini with a T-shirt slung over her shoulder. I'd never had much ambition but right then I'd have done anything to keep her. I chased after her, grabbed her around the waist and swore that we'd leave together and never return.

'Promise?' she laughed.

'I promise. I'm ready to go whenever you want.'

She hung her arms around my neck and dragged me into the dunes.

It took about two months for our plan to fall apart. I found myself on remand after a bad fight with Bulle Hughes outside The Pioneer hotel. We were both drunk and Bulle was just as willing as I was. But seeing as he won himself a broken nose, a cracked eye socket and coughed up a couple of his own teeth, I ended up in court facing a rack of charges. My mother couldn't come up with the bail money and I spent six weeks before the trial in lock-up. China didn't visit once.

When my mother came to see me a couple of days before the trial, carrying a secondhand suit she'd picked up at the Salvos, she broke the news that China had left town and nobody'd heard a word from her. Although her parents reported her missing, and apparently looked sad and sorry enough when they sat in the front pew at church on Sundays, the word was out that her old man had given her money to get away from both me and the town.

As my mother broke the news to me, sighing here and there, I understood I'd let a jewel slip through my fingers.

★

With luck I wasn't accustomed to I beat the assault charges on account of the CCTV footage from the pub showing Bulle whacking me over the head with a billiard cue and trying to gnaw my ear off. Fortunately, there was no footage of me beating him senseless once we'd taken the fight outside. I was free to walk the streets of the town again, which left Bulle a little nervous. He avoided me for weeks. By the time I caught up with him I didn't have the anger to break wind. We passed each other on the footpath out front of the post office. I nodded, he nodded, and that was it.

I asked around about China. Nobody'd sighted her or heard a peep. She'd done a serious runner. Maybe interstate. By the time I went inside again, two years later, for a handful of smash and grabs on servos, I'd been shacked up with three or four local girls, and moved about myself, chasing whatever dollar I could get my hands on. Clean or dirty, it made no difference to me, although if I were pushed I'd have to say dirty money smelt a little better. I would think of China now and then, mostly when I was near the ocean and could smell the sea and salt air.

My first night alone in the narrow prison cell I was kept awake by a sad moaning calling me from across the yard. I didn't sleep that night, and many of the nights that followed. I kept to myself in prison and wasn't troubled at all, but it didn't stop me hitting the mattress full of a fear I couldn't recognise. Some nights I wouldn't sleep at all, and when I did I would dream about China. I'd be searching for her in the darkness, but could never find her.

I left prison a year and a half later with a travel pass, fifty dollars in my pocket and a knitted red rug tucked under my arm that I'd made in the tapestry shop. A gift for my mother. I looked out the bus window at the dots of sheep on the side of a rich green hill, knowing I had fuck all to return to. I didn't have a place to live and my mother was uneasy about me moving in with her. While I was away she'd finally shacked up with her longtime boyfriend, Bob Cummings, a weed of a fella who ran the supermarket. They weren't married, which even in this day is enough to cause scandal in a town with more churches than pubs. The talk around the town worried him and he suggested they get married. My mother wouldn't hear of it.

'I've been married. And it was a disaster from day one. If I wanted a life of misery, Bob, I'd will myself a stroke.'

She'd always been a tough woman. But she wasn't rock-hard. She talked Bob into letting me stay with them and he okayed it for me to move into the garage, which meant his precious fishing boat was shifted onto the driveway, in the weather. I did my best to stay out of his way and only went into the house for meals and to shower. I also made an agreement with them that as soon as I found a permanent job I'd be on my way.

The deal on my early release included me seeing a parole officer once a fortnight and finding work. The week after I got out I caught the bus out front of the post office to the nearest big town, a thirty-minute ride, to have a meeting with my parole officer, Jim Lack. He doubled as a JP, Protestant Minister, and a newsagent. Jim sat me down in a small office behind his shop and assured me that it was his job to set me on the right path. He had the features of a budgerigar and whistled like one when he spoke.

'We're going to work together, son. The last thing we want to see is a local boy falling through the cracks and going back to prison.'

He smiled and put a hand on my thigh, a little too familiar for my liking. He also gave me the number of a 'good Rotary man' he was friendly with who owned a timber mill outside town. When I went for the job interview with the Rotary man, Reg Ling, I quickly worked out that the two men shared a trait other than the Bible and good deeds when he put his hand on my thigh and gave it a good rub.

'I like what I see in you, Cal,' he smiled, like we were on our first date.

★

I started work at the mill a week later, riding an hour each way on an old pushbike I'd picked up at the local tip. I'd spent the weekend taking the bike apart, repairing and cleaning and oiling it. After a week at the mill I sat at the kitchen table with my mother, explaining that if she could have a word in Bob's ear and get him to let me stay in the garage for a little longer than he'd expected, maybe three months or so, rent-free, I'd be able to save enough money to get a place of my own to rent. She agreed, but cut a tough deal with me.

'I don't think he'll mind, Cal. But if you miss just one day of work, or if you bring any trouble here, if the police get on your tail, you'll have to go. Bob won't stand for trouble.'

I felt like screaming, 'Fuck old Bob,' but knew better.

'I understand that. I want no trouble with Bob. Or you.'

From the day I got out of prison I hadn't had another dream about China, although I did think about her a lot of the time I was riding to and from the mill, seeing as it was the same road we'd walked heading for the dunes. I tried convincing myself that the footprints I sometimes spotted in the sand by the side of the road could only be hers. I had a half-crazy idea to take to the road and go searching for her but my parole conditions didn't allow for it. Not for another year, at least. I couldn't venture more than fifty kilometres from the town without written permission, and it was illegal for me to spend a single night away from my 'primary residence,' even just camping out on Bob's front nature strip in a tent.

I'd never driven a forklift before but picked it up in less than a day at the mill. My job was moving sawn and dressed logs from the mill to the storage yard. About fifty men and half a dozen women worked at the mill, a few of them from the town, but most off surrounding farms that had become unproductive in recent years because of the drought. They were an unfriendly bunch. None of them ever introduced themselves or spoke to me any more than they needed to. I guess it was on account of me having been in prison, although they didn't seem to have much to say to each other either.

There was one fella in the mill who looked a little familiar from the first time I spotted him, marking up sawn logs with a brush and bucket of red paint. After that I'd often notice him eyeing me too closely. I'd always been good at putting a name to a face and it got to me that I couldn't remember his. He could be an old enemy who might get it in his head to jump me.

Riding home into the third week on the job, I took a puncture in the back wheel. I had no spare tube or repair kit and was still a good way from home. There wasn't any choice but to walk the bike. Pushing it along the side of the road I heard a car horn. A battered red utility pulled up alongside me, driven by the familiar face from the mill.

'Your bike fucked?' he yelled.

'Yep. A puncture.'

'Throw it in the back and I'll drive you to town.'

I put the bike in the back and hopped into the passenger seat. He offered me a calloused hand.

'Never thought you'd get back here, Cal.'

'I know you?'

'Of course you fucken know me. Bruce Conlan. From high school.'

I remembered Bruce Conlan as a whippet of a kid who smelled of piss and hid himself down the back of the classroom. We'd never been mates, but I'd felt a little sorry for him and had given a couple of boys a belt for standing over him in the yard. He had a lunatic for an old man, who was forever knocking his kids around. While I was in prison I read in the newspaper that the father'd gone berserk in the main street and shot up some shop windows before turning the gun on himself and blowing his head off.

Bruce had filled out. And none of it was muscle.

'I wouldn't have known you, Bruce. You've changed.'

'Well, they say married life's good for you, but I don't know. She can cook, my wife. And I can shovel it away. You look fit enough though. Did you throw the weights around while you were in … in …'

'I never lifted a finger in prison. Didn't eat much either. What you see here is skin and bone and not much more.'

We turned onto the town road.

'Cal, when we were in school together and you cleaned up those arseholes picking on me all the time, I never thanked you for that. No one has laid a finger on me since. They must have thought we were connected. So, thanks.'

'It was nothing.'

'Why'd you do it, stick up for me?'

'Anything for a fight,' I laughed.

He dropped me at the front gate and offered to pick me up of a morning, which suited me, as the bike was on its last legs.

We had little to do with each other during the days at the mill, but did plenty of talking on the drive to and from. Bruce had married one of the Marston girls, the daughters of the same Marstons who ran the milk tankers between the dairy farms and the biggest milk producer in the district, a business they also had a slice of. The family was loaded.

Bruce said his father had rubbed his hands together when he started dating Shelley Marston.

'You'll land on your feet there, son. That family bleeds milk and shits money.'

Bruce hadn't quite landed yet. The family was sweating on the old man dying.

'Still got his first quid in his pocket. Gives his kids fuck all. They hate him and can't wait to bury him.'

'I heard about your old man knocking himself off in the main street. Tough on you?'

'Wasn't tough at all. I was glad to see the mad cunt dead. And happy he never took anyone with him. My mum especially.'

He asked if I minded talking about prison. I said no, but assured him there wasn't much to tell. 'You're in your cell fifteen hours a day, staring at the wall.'

'What's the food like?'

'We eat airline food.'

'Airline food? You having me on?'

'It's true. It's a private company that runs the prison. Their other business is catering for the airlines. They run this industrial kitchen out of the prison. We're the slave labour. Our job is making and preparing the food, which we also have to eat. In the same packaging. Saves on washing the dishes. Think of that, Bruce. You've got some businessman tucking into a meal at 30,000 feet cooked by poor cunts like us who can't walk two steps without hitting a brick wall.'

Bruce cackled like an old girl. He couldn't stop himself from laughing and was looking at me kind of weird.

'Wasn't that funny, mate. An' what are you looking at me like that for?'

'I was just thinking.'

'Thinking what?'

He smiled like a goose. 'I was thinking about you and China.'

I shifted in my seat. 'What about us?'

'You two were like Romeo and Juliet for a while there.'

'Maybe we was. Didn't work out for them either.'

'If you don't mind me saying so, Cal, she was the hottest chick in town. I saw her down at the beach a few times in that red bikini she wore. She drove blokes crazy. What a body she had.'

'Yeah,' I shrugged. 'What a body.'

'Most of the girls we went to school with let themselves go. Tribe of kids. Ton of weight. Not that I can talk,' he laughed, grabbing a handful of fat. 'Not that China Doll.'

'She's most likely gone the same way,' I said, hoping I was wrong. 'It's been a long time.'

'But she hasn't, mate. Not her. Not when I last seen her.'

'You saw her? Bullshit.'

'I did. About six months back. I was after a new dog, a heeler, and went through the stock classifieds in *Farmer's Weekly*. I came across some pups for sale, a litter of blues. I gave the number a call and drove the hundred clicks across west to pick it up, at the old Lion Park on the Western Highway.'

'The Lion Park? Those poor scabby cats still there? I thought the bloke who ran the place was done for animal cruelty.'

'He was. He went broke and sold up to this bloke with the dogs. He runs a few horses, some sheep and these heelers that he breeds. When I got there he let the pups run around in the yard so I could get a look at them and pick one. I'm on my hands and knees playing with this pup, a lovely dark blue – Jhedda, that's what I named her – I picked her out of the litter and brought her home. While I'm playing with the dog I hear a screen door slam and this woman comes out of the house holding a mobile phone. It was a call for him. I look up and see China.'

'You sure it was her?'

'Sure I'm sure. She looked a bit heavier. There was a kid running around. I suppose it was hers. But the face, and that red hair and her eyes. It was China, all right.'

'She say anything to you?'

'You didn't know who I was when you saw me, so why would she? I never existed when she lived here, so she wouldn't know me now. Anyway, she didn't really look at me. She handed him the phone and walked back inside. But it was her.'

I didn't say much for the rest of the drive. When he stopped at the gate I sat in the car without moving.

'We're here, mate. You getting off? Or do you want to come out to my place for a good feed?'

'What's the best way over there?'

'Where? My place?'

'No. The Lion Park.'

'Oh. You cut across country. Take the fire road out behind the speedway. It gives you a straight run to the highway. It's about another forty k on from there. You thinking of catching up with her? I'm sure she'd be married to this bloke. They looked pretty homely out there. I can't see him laying out the welcome mat for an old boyfriend a month out of the nick.'

'I'm not driving over there. Just curious. As it is, I got no car. Thanks for the lift.'

Old Bob was standing by the gate waiting for me.

'How much longer you thinking of being with us, Cal? I don't like my boat out in the sun. Or the rain.'

'Oh, not much longer at all, Bob. I'm about to move on.'

I skipped my mother's cooking and lay on top of my bed thinking about what Bruce had said. Just on dark I grabbed my jacket and wallet, left the garage and headed for an old haunt, the car park at the RSL. I walked the aisles and settled on a battered Ford sedan with an unlocked back passenger door. I'd wired the car in less than a minute and was on the road in another thirty seconds. I passed the speedway and turned onto the fire road, driving through the pitch-black night. Pairs of eyes flashed at me from the scrub and from behind trees. A fox raced onto the dirt road carrying the bloodied carcass of a rabbit in its mouth. I felt the left front wheel slam into it, crushing its ribcage. By the time I'd turned onto the highway I'd dodged a dozen more animals and hit maybe two or three, although I couldn't be sure on account of the bumps and divets in the road.

The Lion Park wasn't hard to find. A faded billboard with the face of a roaring lion welcomed visitors. I pulled off the road at the gates. A light burned on the porch of a house at the end of a drive. I left the car and walked. A dog barked and came running from its bed on the porch. It was an aged blue heeler, a little timid. The porch light went on and the door opened.

There was no mistaking China. The shapely silhouette resting against a door post could belong to no one else. Another dog sat by her side.

'Can I help you? This is private property.'

'China,' I croaked, as if someone had shoved a handful of dust in my mouth.

She stepped forward and stood under the porch

light. She was barefoot and wore a floral cotton dress, with her hair tied in a bun. She looked beautiful.

'Jesus, Cal. Is it you?'

I felt shy all of a sudden, like a schoolboy.

'It's me.'

She came down from the porch and walked across the yard.

'Christ. It is you. Let me look. Wow. What are you doing here?' She was a little nervous. 'My husband, he's away at an ag meet. He'll be back soon.'

'I don't want any trouble, China. I was just driving by.'

She raised a hand, the same soft hand she used to rest in the small of my back.

'It's no trouble. It's just that I wouldn't have expected you to show up out of the blue like this. It's been ... four years?'

'A little more.'

'I read about you in the papers. How long have you been ...?'

'About a month. I've been staying back with Mum.'

She looked out to the highway, to where the stolen car was parked.

'You say you were driving by? How did you know where I was?'

'This fella I've been working with, Bruce Conlan, I guess you don't remember him? He bought one of your dogs some time back. We were talking and your name came up and he told me that he'd seen you. I had to come over this way and I thought – only then when I saw the old sign – that I'd call in and see how you are. But like I said, I don't want to cause you any trouble.'

She shifted on her feet, reached behind her head with a hand and pulled a clip from the back of her hair. Her hair dropped, bounced and rested on her bare shoulders.

'Where are you heading to?'

I heard a car engine, turned and spotted headlights at the end of the drive. China nervously smoothed the front of her dress.

'Here's my husband now.'

I had only seconds left to me.

'China, I just wanted to tell you that when I was inside I thought about you. A lot. It sounds stupid but I need to tell you that you were a good person. I never understood that before. I was too wild to know anything when we were going out.'

I scraped my boot in the dirt.

'And I want to also tell you that you were beautiful. You are beautiful.'

'You told me that plenty of times,' she laughed. 'You were pretty nice yourself.'

'No, I was trouble. I've always been trouble.'

'You were not.' She leaned forward and brushed my arm with a fingertip. 'You were sweet. Most of the time.'

The car pulled into the yard and the dogs ran to meet it. The driver hopped out. He was tall and thin and fit looking, full of purpose, and no doubt suspicious of me.

'Can I help you? Is that your car on the highway?'

'I'm working for a farmer over east and he's after one of your working dogs. I was driving this way and I thought I'd call in on the off-chance. I shouldn't have done so. It's late. My apologies.'

He relaxed a little.

'We don't have pups at the moment. It's not the time of year for them. You should have called ahead.'

'Your wife was just explaining to me that they're out of season.'

He kissed China on the cheek.

'Sorry I'm late, Marg. It went on longer than I expected.'

I hadn't heard China called by her proper name since school rollcall. He took out his wallet and handed me a business card.

'Give me a call around December and I'll let you know what we've got. Should have some pups then.' He offered his hand. 'Tom.'

'Bruce,' I answered. I took the card. 'Thanks.'

I stepped back and took a last look at China, arm-in-arm with her husband.

'And thank you, Marg.'

'You too,' she answered, looking down at her bare feet.

I sat in the car for an hour or more. I couldn't get my mind off her. I got out of the car and watched the house. A honeyed glow framed a narrow window on the side of the house. I walked quietly behind a row of apple trees until I reached the window and stood among the trees, listening to my own heavy breaths as I watched China through the window. She stood naked before a mirror, brushing her hair. Her husband lay back on their bed, smoking a cigarette and admiring her until she turned to him.

I walked back along the driveway to the car, gunned the engine and pulled out onto the highway. The country gradually flattened until the dark horizon fell away. Although the air was cold I wound down the window to keep myself from fading away. I could smell the sea in the wind and thought of China and the nights we'd spent in each other's arms. I could see her hair glowing against the moon and hear her laugh.

I didn't want the highway patrol bearing down on me. I turned onto an irrigation road, running flat and hard into the distance. I could see a radio tower, pulsing a beam of red light across the dark sky. I set my bearings for it, as if it were the Star of Bethlehem itself.

THE TOECUTTERS

WE WENT IN SEARCH OF THE BUNKER throughout spring and into the early summer. The story of a wartime underground command centre, secretly built upriver from the city in the event of a Japanese invasion, was well known. I'd never paid it much attention until Red half convinced me that the story was true.

His Pa had taken a fall staggering home from the pub and broken his leg. He was staying at Red's, where Red's mother was taking care of the old man. There were no spare beds in the house, seeing as there were eight kids in the family. Red and his youngest brother, Charlie, gave up their shared bed for their Pa. Charlie was moved out onto the balcony on the dog's couch, the dog ended up in the yard, and Red took the bedroom floor in a sleeping bag. It sounded like an adventure to me, but he wasn't happy about it.

We were down on the riverbank above the falls, watching workers with survey poles and measuring tapes and binoculars hiking across paddocks, marking the ground for the new bridge being built across the river. It was going to link the new freeway, built to connect the city to the faraway suburbs, with the other side of the river. The streets and the houses behind our own had already gone to the bulldozer, replaced by a deep canyon being gouged out by prehistoric-looking bobcats.

I watched as one of the workers stuck his striped pole in the dirt.

'You know that where we're sitting now, it'll be gone soon. Vanished.'

Red wasn't listening. He was busy getting stuck into his Pa.

'You know he farts in bed. And drinks and smokes all night.'

I picked up a chipped piece of sandstone and pitched it towards the water.

'Everyone farts in bed. When you sleep over at my place you fart all night.'

'I do?'

'In your sleep.'

'Okay. So some of us fart in bed. But what about this? When he wants to have a piss, which is about five times a night because he's drinking so much, he swings his legs out of the bed and nearly knocks me out, whacking me in the side of the head with his foot. He aims for the piss–pot, on the floor, not far from my head, without getting to his feet. Most of the piss misses the pot and goes all over the floor. It will soon rot the lino and floorboards, my dad says.'

He picked up a rock and wrapped his fist around it.

'Do you reckon your mum would let me bunk at your place?'

'How long for?'

'I don't know, until the plaster's off his broken leg.'

'I suppose she wouldn't mind. We've got the room. She says she likes it that you say thank you after eating. And the way you take your dirty plate to the sink. I'll ask tonight.'

I brought the idea up at the tea table. My mother was for it, but the old man wasn't happy. He dropped his newspaper on the table.

'That kid eats like a horse. And don't be giving me a sob story about him missing out on a bed. He probably doesn't get a feed in that house. They breed like flies over there. How many kids are there?'

He was shitty enough, without me asking for a bed for Red. He worked in the foundry at Ruwolt's and the Iron Workers Union had called a go-slow so he wasn't picking up penalties. They were due to call a walkout, which meant he'd be getting no pay except a few dollars from the strike fund. My dad enjoyed a drink and a quiet punt, and unless he was holding out, which wasn't likely, judging by his mood, he'd quickly be broke. Mum always had money put away. That would get us through. But she'd hand it out like a slow dripping tap. There'd be no play money for him, and an extra mouth to feed wouldn't help.

To the old man's relief Red didn't come to stay. That same night, after he'd gone to bed on the floor and his Pop asked him what he'd been up to during the day, Red talked to him about our love for the river and the long days we spent walking its banks and swimming in it when it was warm. His Pop had sat up in bed, downed the dregs of a glass of beer and told a river story of his own.

'You know the old pump house behind the cotton spinners there, just below the waterfall?'

'Yeah, I know it. Me and Joe and some others hang out there when it's wet. We dragged an old couch down there last year. Rolled it down the bank.'

'True? A mate of mine ran the swy game down there for years on Sunday mornings. They'd haul a couple of barrels of beer down there and put on some meat. There'd be hundreds of them, from big punters from the track to a couple of old boys who'd lived in a shack along the bank since the Depression days, all wagering pennies. What a life them boys had. Never worked a day in their life. And out of choice. Except for a bit of labouring they did down there on the shovel during the war.'

Red's ears pricked up just as his Pa was reaching into his underpants to have a good scratch of his balls.

'At the river? What work did they do?'

'Roll us a smoke, son, and I'll tell ya. I have to take a leak.'

'I'll roll a smoke, as long as you keep your aim and don't piss on my head.'

Red rolled two cigarettes, a stock for the old man and a whippet for himself, and lit them both. The old man took a deep puff on his rollie, coughed up some phlegm and spat it into the piss-pot.

'They helped build some sort of air-raid shelter down there. The Americans were holed up at Victoria Barracks near Princes Bridge. Had some sort of speed-boats tied up under the bridge. The idea was that if the Japs attacked they'd jump in the boats and head up the river as far as they could. Couldn't get above the falls, of course. They say they picked a spot this side of the falls and dug into the bank with pick and shovel. Couldn't get heavy machinery down there. It would have got bogged.'

Red took a drag on his cigarette and dropped it into his grandfather's empty beer glass.

'Do you think them old river boys were putting on a

story? People have been talking about that war bunker for years and years. Looking for it too. If it had been built someone would have found it by now, wouldn't they, Pa?'

His Pa picked up a half bottle of beer in one hand and a glass in the other. He held the glass up, looked at the soggy butt sitting in the bottom and shook his head. He put the glass on the floor and took a long swig at the bottle.

'Maybe.' He burped loudly and followed with a trombone fart. 'My body's a fucken symphony, I tell you, son.'

Red tried getting him back on track.

'If there had been a shelter down there, wouldn't they have found it by now?'

'Maybe not. You're talking near thirty years back. All the weeds and shit that have grown up along there since, all the rubbish washed from upriver. Fucken stolen cars dumped and old machinery pushed out the back of the cotton spinners and thrown down the bank. Anything could be under all that. Look long and hard enough and you'll come across the *Titanic*.'

Red knocked at my door early the next morning to report what his Pa had told him. My father opened it, on his way out to work.

'You're early Red. Travelling light. No bags?'

'What?'

'You got a clock at your place? Joe's still in bed.'

Red dodged him, ran up the stairs and charged into my room to tell me the story.

I wasn't convinced about the old river boys' story, but went along. It was winter, not warm enough to swim, and we had nothing better to do. We decided on a plan that we would search the bank from the Johnston Street Bridge to the falls. We'd walked the same bank around a million times and had never spotted evidence of the bunker. I didn't expect that to change.

The bank was covered in a thick mat of weeds, mostly wild fennel and morning glory, from the water's edge to the dirt track running behind the cotton spinners' red-brick wall high above the bank. I wasn't too happy getting in among the weeds, on account of the nesting river rats. Red came up with the idea of tucking the bottoms of our jeans into football socks and wrapping electrical tape around them to stop the rats climbing up our legs. We also carried a golf club each. Red had a three-iron and me a heavy wood. His older brother, Corey, had stolen a set of clubs from the boot of a car, and hadn't been able to sell them off in any of the pubs, with the game of golf being a bit of a mystery where we were from.

The first morning of the search was pissing with rain. As I waded into the bed of weeds I heard the squealing rats scattering about beneath me. Red claimed he couldn't hear a sound but wasn't worried anyway.

'One of them water rats shows its head and I'll fucken club it to death.'

'But what if it gets its teeth into you before you get to it? My old man reckons there's enough poison on the end of a rat tooth to kill a family.'

Red jabbed me in the guts with his club, like it was a sword.

'I'll knock its teeth out of its mouth before it can get near me.'

'Bet you don't'

'Oh, I fucken will. Just watch me.'

We walked on, towards the bridge and poked at the ground with our golf clubs. It didn't take long before we found stuff – bits of rusted machinery, old bottles, a KEEP OUT sign and the skeleton of an animal. I'd seen dead rats before, and another time a bag of rotting kittens in a hessian sack dumped in our lane. I don't know why, but I was more afraid of a dead animal than a living one.

I didn't want to touch the skeleton and called out to Red, who had walked on ahead of me. He came back and pulled the skeleton away from the weeds tangled through its bones.

'What do you think it is?' I asked, standing a good way back. 'It looks like a dog.'

'Na. It's a fox, I'd bet. Look at that bit of red fur on its back. And those teeth. They're longer than a dog's. What do you want to do with it?'

'Nothing. Come on, let's keep going.'

He held the skeleton up by its ribcage. The bones from one of its back legs fell away.

'You sure? We could take it home and make a necklace from its teeth.'

'Fuck off. We're taking it nowhere. If I take that stinking thing near my place my mum will kick my arse.'

Red sniffed along the animal's back, where tufts of fur hung on its backbone.

'It don't smell of nothing.'

'You can't smell it because you've got so much snot up your nose. Get rid of it.'

Red chucked the skeleton into the weeds and ran after me. We reached the bridge having found only more rubbish. We were out of puff and stopped and rested against the bonnet of a burnt-out wreck that had been dumped and set on fire months back. There were another two burnt-out skeletons, a HJ Holden and a VW resting under a span of the bridge. The Council tow-truck came along the track every few months and hauled the wrecks away to the local tip, a few bends along the river.

Red and me shared a cigarette and watched the surveyors working on the other side of the river. He jumped onto the bonnet of the car wreck and used it as a trampoline. A cracking noise bounced off the sandstone cliffs on the other side of the river and shot back to us. The workers stopped and looked over at us, and a flock of cockatoos lifted from a gum tree. They squawked and screeched at Red to cut it out. He went on jumping and giggling to himself until he landed badly and slipped off the bonnet onto the dirt.

'You know you're the dumbest cunt I've ever met,' I told him.

He sat up. The palms of his hands were grazed and muddy and bleeding.

'That's why you hang around with me, Joe, because you're an even dumber cunt. If you knocked around with anyone else you'd get picked on all the time, you're so dumb. You'd be the team fuckwit. You know the spastic kid with the Coke-bottle glasses who lives on top of the milk bar? The one who catches the Special Bus to Special School? If you knocked around with him, Joe, he'd be declared a national fucken genius. That's how dumb you are. I make you look good. Don't you forget that.'

'Oh, I won't Red. I'm forever grateful that my best friend is a self-declared mental case.'

'And a loyal mental case. Don't forget that.'

One of the men was looking through his binoculars at another worker way off in the distance, holding one of the striped poles. I looked upriver to the falls and reminded Red of what I'd tried explaining to him a few days earlier.

'You know all this will be gone soon?'

'The falls? They can't take the falls away.'

'Maybe not the falls. But most everything else. My old man says that they're going to bulldoze the cotton spinners and get rid of the bank on this side of the river and change its direction so the bridge across the river can go in. And they're going to fence it off. He says they'll put a fence along here with barbed wire across the top and we won't be able to get down to the river from this side at all. We'll have to go the long way, around to the other side where all the rich people live.'

'Bullshit. They can't change the river like that and put a fence up. This is our river.'

He put his hands to his mouth and screamed at the top of his voice across the water to the workers.

'Fuck off. This is our river.'

One of them yelled back, 'Fuck off yourself,' and they all laughed.

'They are changing it, you'll see. The government can do anything they want. They don't care about you and me. Look at them houses behind us that they knocked down. None of them live here, and don't give a fuck.'

'We'd better get on with it then.'

'Get on with what?'

'Finding the bunker. Before it gets blown to smithereens by these cunts.'

We searched for months for the bunker, the nights after school and on weekends. We'd come home at the end of a day's exploring soaked through with rain and covered in mud. I knew we'd never find it, and so did Red, I'm sure. But neither of us said so. We were having too much fun, spending all the time we could with the river before it changed forever. And each day the canyon being dug for the foundations of a bridge that would cross the river moved closer to the water.

In the last week before the end of the school year I was asleep in bed early one morning when I was woken by a knock at the window. I turned from my side to my back and the sound came again. I crawled out of bed and opened the blind. Red was standing in the middle of the street wearing a pair of pyjama shorts and a singlet and was throwing pebbles at my window.

'What are you doing, Red? You piss the bed?'

'No. That's my Pa's job. Get down here. There's cops everywhere.'

'Cops? Where?'

'Out the back. Where the hole's been dug. There's TV people there too. I'll meet you at your back gate.'

I grabbed some clothes from the floor, pulled my jeans on and ran down the stairs with a pair of runners in my hand and a T-shirt over my shoulder. Red was standing by the gate. Behind him were police, TV news cameras and a crowd. A policeman was knocking a metal picket into the earth. He tied a length of rope to it and paced out the ground until he'd decided on a second spot to bang in another picket. When he'd finished he tied the length of rope to the second picket, stood guard in front of it and ordered the crowd to stand back.

Red clapped his hands together like he was at a football game.

'Whoa, Jo-ey. This looks serious. Let's get a better look.'

He was off before I had my shoes on. The ground was sticky with mud. By the time I got to the roped-off area my shoes were black. Red was in the ear of Telegram Simms, who, at around the age of eighty, was the oldest paperboy in the world. He knew everything. They say he broke the Kennedy assassination before Oswald had fired a shot.

'A dead body? You sure?' Red asked. He turned to me and whispered, 'Joey. It's a body, Telegram says. In the ditch just there. He says someone was shot.'

'How's he know?'

'Same way he always knows.'

'And what's that?'

'Mental telepathy. My old man says that Telegram is gifted.'

'Maybe he should get a proper job then.'

Word about the shooting spread quick as lightning. The crowd got bigger as people waited for the body to be brought up from the ditch. I listened in on one of our neighbours, Kitty Marsh, talking to a policeman. She said that the shooting had taken place somewhere else and the body had been dumped.

'I would've heard a shotgun going off. I haven't slept through the night in over ten years. I wake to the heartbeat of an ant.'

The policeman looked at her suspiciously.

'Who told you it was a shotgun?'

'Well, Telegram there just said that half his face is missing. It's got to be either a shotgun or a cannon ball.'

The crowd hushed as two men in grey coats struggled through the mud with a stretcher carrying a lumpy body bag. Police ran ahead of the stretcher and held the crowd back until it had passed through. It was placed on a slide-out tray in the back of a van with darkened windows. A police car pulled in front of the van, turned its siren and flashing blue light on and took off with the van close behind. It was only then that the crowd thinned.

We talked about the dead body on our way to and from school that day. Red thought it was probably a cheating husband who had been caught with another woman.

'How could you know that?'

'I've been watching *Divorce Court* on the TV, with my mum and sisters, and there's a lot of cheating husbands. Everywhere.'

'And you think that a wife could blow her husband's head off and dump him here? Drag him through all that mud. I don't think so.'

'No. Not the wife. Maybe a husband who's been cheated on. Revenge. My Pa says that if a man wants to get himself in trouble, serious trouble, he cheats with another man's wife or girlfriend. Says it's more dangerous than doing a bank job.'

'And when does he pass on gems like that? While you're watching *Divorce Court*?'

'Yep. We have to tell him to shut up so we can hear.'

That afternoon Red's Pa was sitting on the front verandah in a broken lounge chair catching the sun. He held up the newspaper.

'Hey ya, boys? It was Dessie Sharp.'

'Who was?' Red asked.

'The stiff in the hole. Desmond Arthur Sharp. A robber.'

'Bank robber?'

He dropped the newspaper onto his lap.

'Anything. Banks. And pubs. Gambling joints. Dessie wasn't fussy. He'd rob his mother if she were holding. His face is gone. They identified him through a tattoo on his arm – *Death Before Dishonour* – he must have been a comedian. He wouldn't know what honour was.'

I tried reading the headline.

'Does it say why he was murdered?'

'Well, sort of. There was a big robbery in Sydney only a few weeks back, one of the biggest ever. Says in the paper it was a Melbourne crew. A hit-and-run job. Dessie was one of the suspects, it says here.'

Red scratched at his chin.

'But that doesn't tell you why he was murdered, does it?'

'No. But it don't take much to put two and two together.'

'Which adds up to what, Pa?'

'The Toecutters, of course. Has to be.'

Red and me gulped at the same time. While nobody had ever laid eyes on them, everyone had heard of the Toecutters, a criminal gang that made their living torturing other robbers, after an armed robbery on a bank or TAB. If the robbers didn't hand over their takings they had their toes cut off, fingers and maybe an ear or a nose.

'Does it say in there if this fella, Dessie, has some toes missing?' Red asked.

'Not yet. But don't worry, it'll come out later. The coppers might hold it back. They do that. There'll be grief over this. Dessie won't be the only cab off the rank.'

Red's mother came out of the house. She was wearing an apron and holding a walking stick in one hand.

'Stop filling these kids with stories, Dad. Come on, inside. You too, Redmond.' She waved the stick at me. 'You get on home, Joseph. Your mother will be worrying over you.'

Red took the stick from his mother, handed it to his Pa and helped him to his feet. She had a fierce look on her face.

'Are you going, Joseph?'

'Yeah, I'm going.'

As soon as she'd walked back inside the old man was at it again.

'Don't listen to your mother, Red. This is no story. I'd bet my pension he won't be the only one cut loose. There's big money involved in this. And it'll be play for keeps.'

The dead man was named in the newspaper a few days later, just as Red's Pa had said, as 'a key suspect in a major armed robbery'. He was also missing a big toe from each foot and had some broken fingers. I was around at Red's the next night, sitting with his Pa while his parents were out at the 50–50 dance, when a newsflash interrupted the episode of *Tell The Truth* we were watching. A skinny-looking fella wearing a suit and tie and standing in the middle of a street in Carlton reported that a woman had phoned the police two days earlier to tell them that three men wearing balaclavas had chopped her front door down with an axe and dragged her boyfriend into a car with a sawn-off shotgun at his head.

The dead man's name was James 'Rabbit' Patterson. He was 'known to police', and hadn't been seen since the abduction.

Red looked at me, rolled his eyes and turned to his Pa, sitting on the couch, necking a bottle.

'What do you think of that, Pa? What's it mean?'

'Well, it figures. The Rabbit runs with a different crew. And he's always used an over-and-under, and not a side-by-side.'

'What's that mean? An over-and-under?'

'Don't be asking me. Your mother's already got the shits about this. We're not to talk of this again. She's warned me off. I don't want to be turfed out of here.'

'Come on, Pa. She won't be home for ages. What's it mean? We won't say anything will we, Joe?'

'Nothing,' I added.

He rested his beer bottle on the floor.

'Well, they're both double-barrels and if they hit you direct they do pretty much the same job. But the over-and-under's always been the favourite for a head shot.'

He picked up the bottle of beer, toasted no one in particular and downed it.

'Dessie was shot in the head, and the Rabbit's signature was an over-and-under. And now he's off too. Case solved.'

'Where do you reckon he's off to?' I couldn't help asking.

'We won't go there, Joey. I've said enough. Help us up, Redmond.'

'Not until you tell us where he might end up.'

'I hope you're fucken kidding me, son. When I tell you it's enough, it's for your own good. You boys haven't a clue how the street works. Learn quick, before you find yourselves in trouble.'

It was the first time I'd seen menace on the old man's face. He was frightening. Then he smiled and the threat was gone.

'I'm sorry, Pa,' Red said. 'But tell us. Please.'

'You really want to know?'

We nodded.

'Okay. Not a word. They could chop him up into pieces and smuggle him into the fertiliser works they use over in Footscray. Cost them a packet at the gate. But it's worth it. Turn him into blood and bone in around a minute. Do some good in the garden. Or there's the furnace at the glassworks. Been used before. Temperature's so high the body disappears before your eyes, like magic. But my bet, seeing as they'd want to be rid of him straight off, it would have been the river or the bay. Collect him from home, knock him, weigh him down and send him off with a water burial. Quick and simple. But who can be sure? It's like this TV show we're watching, boys. You got three to choose from and two of them are bullshit artists. Take your pick.'

The summer was hot and we swam in the river each day. We'd given up searching for the bunker. It was too hot to be hiking along the banks armed with our golf clubs, and as it was we were bored with the search anyway. There'd been little more news about the murder of Dessie Sharp or the disappearance of Rabbit Patterson. There were whispers about the Toecutters in the pubs and on the street corners, but no talking out of turn to the police, so the police were stuck.

By New Year the digging for the freeway had reached the river. A fence line was marked out along the bank and post holes had been dug. We'd soon be cut off from our regular swimming hole. We sat on the bank above the river on New Year's Eve and watched as the workmen laid out rolls of wire. Red declared that we should sneak down to the river in the night and cut a hole through the fence.

'Fuck them. They can't keep us out.'

'And what will we do when we want a swim? Even if we cut through the fence and get to the water, they'll kick us out anyway, once they spot us. We have to find another place to swim.'

'Why should we? *This* is our place.'

'I know it is. But I want a swim and we can't do it here.'

'Where then?'

'On the other side. Let's walk across the falls and try for a new spot.'

The weir wall above the falls was capped in cement. The river was running low. We walked knee deep across the slimy surface, heading for the far bank. Red struggled like a tightrope walker trying to keep balance.

'Jesus Christ, it's slippery, Joe. If we go over the edge we'll be smashed on the rocks.'

'But we're not going over. Don't look down and keep your eye on the bank.'

We slid and skated our way to the bank without taking a fall. We sat on a sandstone ledge and dangled our feet in the water. It was a nice spot.

'We can't swim below the falls. It runs too fast and the water's too shallow. But,' I pointed to a dead tree upstream, leaning badly towards the water, 'just there, where the cliff drops into the water, it's calm and should be deep. There's a diving spot and we could hitch a rope to the tree.'

We walked along the sandstone ledge until we were directly above the dead tree. I looked across the river to the other side. A wrecking ball was attacking the red-brick wall of the cotton spinners and a bulldozer worked along the bank below it, clawing at the dirt. Our old swimming hole was a bombsite. I climbed down the sandstone steps and stood at the river's edge. There were plenty of spots to dive or jump from. All we needed was deep water. The dark colour was promising.

I stripped off my T-shirt and slid into the water. I swam away from the bank and trod water, waiting for Red to swim out to me.

'Let's see how deep it is.'

I duck-dived and headed for the bottom. The light faded around me. My ears felt like they were about to burst and I had to surface before touching the bottom. We swam around in a circle, diving again, testing the depth.

It would be safe to jump.

Red perched on one ledge, me on another. On the count of three we lifted off and bombed into the water together. We swam back to the edge, climbed out, and took off again and again. We jumped until we'd worn ourselves out. We shared a ledge and lay in the sun smoking cigarettes, me on my back and Red sitting up. He pointed to the highest point of the ledge.

'Hey, do you think we could jump from up there? Would we clear the bank?'

The ledge was thirty, maybe forty feet above the water.

'You'd have to fly to clear the bank.'

'I could do it. Easy.'

'Easy, my arse. Maybe you can do it, but it won't be easy.'

He stood up and flicked his butt in the air.

'Watch me.'

He scrambled up the ledge and stood with his toes curling over the edge. He swung his arms back and forward like he was about to take off, stopped, and dropped his arms to his side. Just when I thought he'd talked himself out of it he bent at the knees, lifted off and jumped from the ledge, screaming his lungs out and waving his arms about as he fell. Just before he hit the surface he straightened his body and plunged into the water with hardly a splash. He disappeared for a few seconds then popped up again, screaming, 'I hit something, I hit something.'

I looked down and screamed out to him, 'What, the bottom?'

He took a deep breath and duck-dived. I couldn't see him at all in the murky water. The only trace of Red were the bubbles of air escaping from his lungs. He surfaced again, gasped for air and swam for the bank, talking like crazy before he was out of the water.

'There's a car down there. When I jumped I landed on the roof. And when I just went back down I could make out the colour. I'm pretty sure it's white. Or maybe yellow. Wonder when it was put there? Maybe there's someone in it? An accident or something?'

'What sort of car?'

He pulled himself out of the water and sat at my feet.

'What do you mean, what sort?'

'You know, what make? It could've been down there for years.'

'What make? How the fuck would I know? I'm not a car dealer. I can hardly see a thing down there. Come take a look.'

He waded back into the water, swam out and dived again. I was about to follow him when I suddenly thought about Rabbit Patterson and the watery grave Red's Pa had mentioned. I climbed up the ledge, away from the water, sat down and waited. Red dived a couple more times before coming back to the bank and climbing out.

'Come on in, you lazy cunt. This is like Jacques what's-his-name. We should get some goggles or a mask or something and take a better look.'

'Maybe we shouldn't be looking too close, Red.'

'Why not?'

'Because of the Rabbit. Remember what your Pa said.'

'The Rabbit? What's this got to do with the ...' the penny dropped. 'Fuck me, Joe. The Rabbit. You think he might be down there, in the car?'

'Why not? He could be. His car went missing with him. Said so in the paper.'

'What make of car was it? Did they describe it in the paper?'

'They did.'

'And?'

'A white Valiant. They said it was a white '64 Valiant.'

'Fuck me.'

One minute Red was ordering me around, reminding me not to say a word to anyone about the car, and the next minute he'd decided we should call the police. He'd taken to the new swimming hole and didn't like the idea of sharing it with a rotting corpse.

'We don't know that there's a body down there.'

'You mightn't know, but I've got a feeling about this, Joe. I'm sure there's a body down there. And even if there's not, that car will start bleeding oil soon and we won't be able to swim here.'

We gathered our clothes and cigarettes and headed back across the falls. We left the river, walked to the public telephone box at the railway station and tossed a coin to decide who would report the car. I'm not sure if you would call it a win or a loss, but Red correctly called heads and decided I was going to make the call. I took my T-shirt off and covered the receiver to disguise my voice, just like I'd seen on an episode of *Homicide*. I dialled 000 and waited.

'Police, Fire or Ambulance?'

'Police,' I growled.

I heard a click, a hissing sound and then a voice.

'Victoria Police. Russell Street.'

I tried so hard to change my voice the policeman on the other end of the line couldn't understand what I was saying and had to ask me to repeat myself. Either that or it was a trick and he was putting a trace on the call. I talked faster, telling him that the body of the missing man, Rabbit Patterson, was in the boot of his own car, at the bottom of the river, above the falls.

When he asked me for my name and address I hung up.

'We better take off, Red. If they trace the call to us we're history.'

'Wipe your prints off first, with the T-shirt.'

We ran back to the river and hid in the old pump house, directly across the river from the ledge we'd

45

jumped from. We had a good view through a broken window.

'Do you reckon they'll come?' Red asked.

'Should do. They've been looking everywhere for him. This is a gift.'

'Did it sound like the copper you were talking to believed you?'

'Yeah. I think so. I could hear a tap-tap noise like he was typing out what I said. And he asked me about the spot three times. *Can you repeat the location of the vehicle, sir?* He said it like that. Official.'

It was well after dark before we gave up waiting.

'I'd better get home, Red, or I'll get my arse kicked.'

'Me too. We'll have to get back here early in the morning. I want to be here when they bring him up.'

'I can't be here. I have to go to church. My cousin's Communion. They probably won't come. Anyway, we don't know if he's down there.'

'I bet he is. Tied and gagged in the boot.'

When I got home from church the next afternoon Red was standing on the street corner, waving like mad at me. When he saw my father spying him he took off around the corner.

'What's he want?' he growled at me. 'He's a hell of a lot of trouble, that boy.'

'No he's not. We're going to go for a hike.'

'A hike? What do you mean, a hike?'

'You know, a walk around the river.'

He shook his head and looked at my mum for support. She shrugged her shoulders.

'Be home before dark,' she warned me. 'And stay out of the water. It's filthy.'

I turned the corner, to where Red was waiting.

'Hurry, Joe. They're down there, now. The coppers with divers with tanks on their backs, going in where we found the car.'

We sprinted all the way to the river and didn't stop until we were in the pump house, sitting at the broken window. I could see a diver in the water holding a large metal hook attached to a heavy length of wire stretching from the water, over the bank, and along the ledge to a tow-truck parked on a track above the river. The diver slipped under the water and reappeared, minus the hook, about a minute later. He hopped out of the water and another copper waved to the tow-truck driver. He jumped into the truck and turned the ignition. Black smoke spluttered from the exhaust as the winch on the back of the truck began to turn. Red and me kept our eyes on the water as the wire groaned against the sandstone ledge and bubbles bigger than beach balls popped and farted on the surface of the water. The tail-light of a car broke through. As it was lifted from the river, water spewed from the open windows until the car was dangling like a white-pointer shark from the end of the line.

Red pushed the window open, squinted into the distance then dropkicked a rusting beer can across the room.

'Fuck. That's not a Valiant. Take a look at the tail-lights, Joe.'

'You're right. It's no Valiant. Maybe an FC Holden?'

'FB.'

'Yeah. FB. Doesn't mean he's not in there.'

'The Rabbit's not in there. They took him away in his own car. They would've dumped him in his own car. Fuck this. I'm off.'

I caught up to him and put my arm on his shoulder as we walked home.

'Hey, take it easy, Red. We've got the best swimming hole along the river, all to ourselves, and a lot of summer left.'

'Not too bad, I suppose,' he smiled. 'What about the bunker?'

'What about it?'

'Maybe it is here. Tomorrow, we start looking for it again. You with me?'

'Yep. I'm with you.'

REFUGE OF SINNERS

IN THE MONTHS AFTER THE FUNERAL Emma and I
avoided each other as much as we could. I spent a
lot of my time in the back garden raking fallen leaves
and weeding the garden beds, jobs I'd never bothered
with before. She buried herself under a blanket in the
old armchair in the spare room at the other end of
the house. Dinner times were the hardest. We'd always
eaten together as a family. The kitchen table was where
we came together at the end of the day and talked and
argued and laughed. But no longer. She made a point
of feeding the kids early, alone. I didn't sit down to eat
at all. When I did get hungry I picked at whatever was
available – leftovers in the fridge, dry biscuits, sometimes cereal in the early hours of the morning.

One afternoon Emma stood on the back verandah
with a paperback tucked under her arm. I was on
my knees sifting through the rose beds with my bare

hands and spotted her out of the corner of my eye and continued digging. She quietly watched me for a few minutes before walking into the garden.

'I've just spoken to Roger. I've decided I'm going back to work next week.'

I looked over my shoulder at her. The bright sun near blinded me. Emma worked as a lawyer with the Public Advocate's Office, and was one of their most valued workers. When I didn't respond she squatted next to me and rested a hand on my thigh.

'Are you okay with that? I can put it off for another week or two, if you need me here.'

'No. That's fine. Yes, go back.'

I didn't want to tell her that I felt relieved. With her back at work and the kids at school the house would be empty for most of the day and I wouldn't have to speak to anyone at all.

'Are you sure?'

'I'm sure, Em.'

She set the bedside alarm for six, and left the house by seven on the following Monday morning. I heard the front door close and lay in bed listening to Alex and Nina banging around in the kitchen, making breakfast and organising themselves for school. Alex was the eldest. From the day he'd started high school I'd been happy for the children to go their separate ways of a morning. But not any longer, insisting that he drop

Nina at her primary-school gate before heading off on his own.

I waited until I heard their footsteps in the hallway before getting out of bed, and watched from the lounge-room window as they walked out the gate and headed along the street. Nina lagged behind her older brother, who was smacking his basketball against the footpath as he walked. Alex played guard for the school team. He was a genuine talent and loved the game. He carried his basketball wherever he went. He even took it to bed with him.

It was a cool morning and I noticed that Alex was wearing Josh's red parka over his uniform. Although he'd been wearing it all winter without complaint from me, I felt a sudden rise of anger, believing he had no right to the jacket. I rushed from the room and opened the front door, about to scream at him to come back with the jacket. Nina, who must have heard the front door open, spun around on the heels of her school shoes, smiled gently and waved at me. I returned the gesture and kept my eye on her until she'd disappeared around the corner at the end of the street. After they had left for school I had to fight a feeling I was overwhelmed by: that it would be a miracle if they both made it home that night.

I closed the front door and headed for the back garden to retrieve my crumpled packet of cigarettes and box of matches from the darkened corner of the top shelf in the shed. For the next hour or more I sat on the verandah in my pyjamas and dressing gown smoking cigarettes and watching the birds skip from branch to branch in the bare magnolia at the bottom of the garden.

I spent the remainder of the morning on my daily mission, wandering the house, stopping now and then to look at a family photograph in the hallway, or examine a smudged Vegemite fingerprint on a kitchen cupboard door and wonder which one of my children it belonged to. I ended my pilgrimage at the laundry doorway and studied the markings in the wooden frame where I'd recorded the heights of my children on the date of each of their birthdays. Taking my reading glasses out of my dressing-gown pocket I re-read the measurements and dates several times before running my fingertips across the scars in the wood.

I'd be exhausted by lunchtime and would find my way to Josh's room and his bed, where I'd lie looking up at the fine web of cracks in the ceiling that had been there since we bought the house fourteen years earlier. I'd never got around to repairing them. I never slept for long, maybe an hour or so. After getting up to leave the bedroom I'd look over my shoulder at the hollow I'd left behind.

My days alone were occupied with the same activity – exploring the house, shuffling from room to room and rummaging through cupboards, bookshelves and storage boxes. Most of what I came across I'd already discovered, weeks earlier – until the morning I discovered the glass jar wedged between the back of the leather couch and the wall. I sat on the couch and nursed the jar in my arms. It was sealed tight after being filled with hundreds of pieces of beach glass and topped with seawater. Each piece of glass had been slowly worn smooth by sand and surf, pounded in the rhythm of the sea.

The jar was covered in a thick layer of dust. As I washed it in the kitchen sink the colours and shapes of glass caught the sunlight streaming through the window. As I lifted the jar out of the soapy water and held it to the light it slipped from my hands and smashed onto the kitchen floor, scattering brown, green and frosted pieces of glass across the tiles. On my hands and knees I began separating out the smooth pieces of beach glass from the jagged remains of the jar. As the scent of the ocean wafted up I thought about the family trips we'd made to the beach each summer, and how the kids would compete to find the most valued pieces of glass – the rare blues and reds.

The task of carefully sifting through the glass seemed overwhelming; demanding concentration, a skill I'd lost. Judging by the amount of dust caked on the jar – it must have been resting under the couch for some time – none of us had missed it. The easiest means of cleaning up would be to tip the lot into the bin. The job would be over in minutes.

Armed with the brush and pan from under the sink, I was about to sweep the mess away when a piece of glass caught my eye. Holding it between my finger and thumb I thought about which one of the kids had collected it. Perhaps it was one of Emma's finds? Or mine? I meticulously gathered each piece of glass in a colander, rinsed it under the kitchen tap and left it to drain in the sink. In the garden I searched through the shed until I found a similar-sized jar to the one I'd smashed. I cleaned it out, emptied the pieces of glass into the jar and filled it with tap water. As I was about to screw the lid down I remembered something and added a couple of spoonfuls of sea salt for effect.

Emma seemed pleased to be back at work and began gently prodding me about when I might return myself. My answer, always the same, 'It could be next week, I think,' was usually enough to stop her prodding further, although I noticed she was becoming frustrated with my self-imposed isolation. I rarely left the house, even avoiding collecting the morning paper from the local newsagent, a task I'd enjoyed most mornings for many years.

I had walked to the newsagency a week after the

funeral and was shocked when Jim, the shop owner, mentioned Josh's name.

'He was my most reliable paperboy, Josh. He was never late. Not once.'

I'd offered him the money for the newspaper without saying a word. He looked me in the eye as he handed me the change.

'We all know it was an accident. It couldn't be helped.'

It couldn't be helped.

It wasn't until I opened a letter from the advertising agency I'd been with for eight years, instructing me that I'd exhausted all my leave entitlements, paid and unpaid, that I reluctantly agreed to an appointment with my manager, Ron Hartlett. I called his secretary and told her I'd come in the following day. I burned the letter in the old incinerator in the garden along with the leaves I'd been raking up, and didn't mention the letter or the meeting to Emma that night. I watched on, with the birds flittering around me, disturbed by the flames and smoke.

The next morning I waited for Emma to leave then showered and left the house myself about five minutes behind the kids, catching the train into the city for the first time in months. I sat across the aisle from two teenage boys wearing a near-matching uniform of low-slung jeans, scuffed sneakers and hooded windcheaters. They each carried a skateboard. I lowered my head and looked down at my own dusty leather shoes and eavesdropped on their conversation. The boys were talking excitedly about a skating spot they were heading to behind the football stadium at Docklands. As they stood up to get off the train, one stop before my own, I almost reached out and touched one of the boys on the arm as he passed by.

I walked from the station to my office building. Certain that I'd been called in to be told I was going to get the sack, I'd written and signed a resignation letter the previous afternoon. It was without fuss, just two short sentences. Ron Hartlett, my direct line manager, had been with the Melbourne office for little more than a year. The word around the corridors prior to his arrival was that he was a tough nut who'd been brought down from head office in Sydney 'to kick a few arses and clear the place of deadwood'.

While nobody's arse had been kicked, not as far as I knew, I felt nervous when his secretary ushered me into his office that morning. Sinking into the leather chair opposite him I immediately worried about how I would ever get to my feet again.

'Nick. Would you like a tea or coffee?' he offered.

'No. That's no bother.'

He looked a little embarrassed and nervous himself. Before he could say anything more I fumbled for the envelope in my jacket pocket and passed it across the desk to him. After reading it he carefully folded the letter, returned it to the envelope and placed it between us on the desktop. He rested his hands behind his head and closed his eyes. I glanced out of the window, at a magpie sitting on the ledge high above the city. It looked back at me as it pecked at the glass.

Eventually Ron picked up the envelope again and gently tapped it on the desktop as he spoke.

'Nick, I would like to hold onto this if you don't mind. Can I suggest you give some thought to working from home? We could begin with a day or two a week until you're ... comfortable. You can send material in from home. If you can get to the monthly team meetings, that's all we'd need, for now.'

He passed the letter across the desk to me.

'I'm not saying I won't accept this. It's your decision and I respect it. But I'd like us to revisit this later, if we need to.'

He took his glasses off, held them to the light and studied the lenses. The room suddenly felt warmer and I was beginning to sweat and I couldn't decide if I wanted to take my jacket off or run from the room and out of the building. I was about to stand up and excuse myself when Ron put his glasses back on and cleared his throat. He picked up a photograph that was sitting on the bookshelf behind his desk. It was a picture of an attractive-looking woman around the same age as Emma.

'My wife died of cancer three years ago. She'd been sick for several years. It may not be quite the same, but I do know that it takes time when you lose someone ...'

He sat upright in his chair. I wanted to say something but the words were stuck in my throat. I looked out at the ledge for the bird. It was gone. 'It was an accident,' I eventually croaked. What I'd said made no sense to me, so I didn't expect him to understand. I prised myself from the chair, hurriedly excused myself and left the office.

I talked to Emma about the meeting later that night as she sat in bed reading.

'What meeting? You didn't tell me about a meeting,' she questioned.

'I forgot.'

'Forgot?' she frowned. 'So, will you take up his offer, to work from home?' She hesitated. 'I think it would be good for you.'

She took hold of my hand, squeezed it tightly and smiled. I felt guilty. She was holding the family together on her own.

*

I sent a couple of projects into the office over the following weeks, and was invited to the next monthly meeting. Again I took the train into the city and had every intention of turning up at the meeting. As I was standing on the escalator, leaving the underground station, I looked up at the square of open sky above me and was struck with a familiar sense of anxiety. I grasped the front of my shirt and rested against a lamppost at the intersection across the street from my building. I waited on the corner and watched as the lights changed several times. Eventually I turned around and headed in the opposite direction from the office.

I walked the streets of the city, occasionally stopping to look at a shop window display, eventually finding myself outside Bernard's Magic Shop on Elizabeth Street. My father had taken me there with my older brother, Christopher, when we were small boys. Like most children, I was mesmerised by magic, while Chris was ever the cynic. I'd once been at a magic show at the local town hall. He'd been sitting behind me with a couple of mates, and had leaned across and screamed in my ear, 'It's only a trick, Nicky; it's all a trick. None of this is true.'

I'd felt betrayed by what he'd said. He'd robbed me of something precious and I never forgave him.

My stomach began rumbling. I was hungry, but had been too nervous to eat breakfast that morning and had eaten nothing since. I walked past several crowded cafés before choosing one that had only single bar stools in the front window. Inside, I ordered a sandwich, ate quickly and left.

Returning to the train station I heard the ringing of church bells above the noise of city traffic. The sound reminded me of the bell that hung atop the Catholic church a few streets from my childhood home. The bell would ring out each weekday morning announcing eleven o'clock mass, and four times on Sundays, once for each mass. Although my parents were not religious they insisted on sending Chris and me to the Catholic school next to the church, to 'keep us in order', my father claimed. He dragged us from our beds early on Sunday mornings, forcing us to nine o'clock mass and a front pew, where we would be sure to catch the eye of the nuns who taught us.

I followed the sound of the bells across Elizabeth Street and stopped in front of a wrought-iron gate leading into a churchyard, before walking through the darkened wood-panelled entrance of the church. Although mass was not being said the church was almost full. I rested against the back pew and watched as people came and went. Some dropped to their knees and prayed with rosary beads entwined around their clasped hands, while others sat quietly with heads rested in their hands and their eyes closed.

With little understanding of what I was doing, I walked along a side aisle and approached a seat, unable to recall if I was supposed to kneel, make the sign of the cross, or do both. After some confusion I did neither. Although I have only a slight build, as I sat down I felt the full weight of my body. The oak pew creaked loudly in response. Feeling weary, I rested my head against the back of the pew and looked up at the timber panelling in the ceiling above the altar. The inlay of each oak panel had been finished in brightly painted gold stars on a blue background.

I woke to the sound of the church bells, sat up and wiped saliva from my chin. A woman was kneeling next to me, quietly reciting a prayer to herself. She picked at a strand of wool on the sleeve of the cardigan she was wearing. It began to unravel. I stood up, walked back along the aisle and was about to pass by the side nave when I stopped. It was aglow with many hundreds of candles burning on a series of metal tiers on both sides of a small altar. A kaleidoscope of colours projected onto a wall above, the effect of the afternoon sun touching a stained-glass window.

I picked up a candle – it resembled a parched finger bone – and lit its wick from another before placing it on the topmost tier. As I did so the melting wax dripping from the next candle bled onto the back of my hand and scalded my skin. I suddenly felt that I needed to sit again. I looked up at the window, and read the inscription bordering it – *Refuge of Sinners*. I closed my eyes and thought about my son.

THE GHOST OF HANK WILLIAMS

CURTIS PLAYED A DEADLY TWELVE-STRING GUITAR out front of the old Lido Ballroom on Saturday mornings, picking up a few dollars from the market shoppers. He could really sing too, a few years back – country and western, and some blues – but now his voice was shot, along with his body and he just sort of wailed and grunted. The guitar had seen better days, too. He'd been hit over the head with it more than once, mouthing off on the grog. It was flattened one time when Thin Lizzie, one of the girls who worked Banana Alley, serving high and low rollers out of the casino, slipped from a stool in the front bar of the Blue Oyster and landed tits up on the axe.

He'd repaired the guitar over and over with some string, electrical tape and a prayer. There wasn't a musician on earth who could have willed a decent tune out of that guitar after all the abuse it had taken. Except for

Curtis. He could get it to weep like a mother who'd lost a newborn. Some say the rock-hard and ruinous life he'd led had destroyed his playing. I reckon it made him better.

In his younger days there wasn't a drug known to man that Curtis hadn't fallen for. He'd survived his suicidal habits and the pals he'd cut loose with over the years – Big Tiny Johnson, Lenny the Leper and Ringo Moss among them. Big Tiny, all twenty stone of him, could sing like a bird. Him and Curtis had travelled the road and played in every country pub from Melbourne to the Gulf and back, making just enough to keep their wild side cared for, until Big Tiny died in his sleep after a three-day bender on the streets of Sydney.

Curtis had given some of the poison a rest for years but continued his love of the drink. It was an affection we shared. He'd come to terms with some moderation in recent years and had his rules. He never touched a drink on Friday nights and didn't enjoy his first taste of the weekend until the last shoppers had drifted away from the market on a Saturday.

We'd meet up on those afternoons behind the doughnut stand. I'd be carrying some cold beers and a bottle of wine from the bottle-shop across from the market. He'd have the guitar slung across his shoulder and would be licking his lips, anxious for a drop. We'd make our way up to the park and sit under one of them big Moreton Bays that some smart fella had planted a hundred years back to keep the sun off. Curtis loved to talk but conversation with him was sometimes hard to follow. The stories he told roamed back and forward over time. Or he'd pluck a moment from the sky and mash it up with some nightmare he'd had months back when he was in the DTs after a big drink.

'You heard of the Black Elvis, Sammy?' he asked me one time.

'Who's he?'

'Blackfella from up north who can sing and play like fire. But better than that he came out of a rock in the ground. He was a lizard. And now he's a human. He was a rock before.'

'A rock?'

'Other times the sea.'

'He comes from the sea?'

'No. He was the sea.'

I didn't believe most of what Curtis said until I got charged up myself and it all made sense.

I'd tried hard to give up on drink myself. I got a scare one time after this young doctor – said she was from Hong Kong or somewhere – put a picture of my insides against a wall, turned on a light, pointed to my liver and said it was the worst she'd seen in ten years in the business. She stuck another picture on the wall alongside mine.

'See here, Mr Holt?' she said, pointing. 'This is what a healthy liver looks like.'

It looked fat and well fed. 'You're right there, Doc. That's a very healthy liver.' I knew then that I was well and truly fucked.

Poring over the picture of my insides, she screwed up her nose like one of us had farted. 'Now, take a good look at your own liver, Mr Holt. What do you see?'

It looked like a dried-up and burnt old lamb chop that had been left for dead.

'I'm not sure, Doc. I don't have your experience, you see?'

She sat me down and told me straight that if I didn't get off the drink I'd likely be dead in six months, cranking the story with a mess of scare tactics to frighten me off. I forgave her good intentions. After all, she was a doctor.

'Do you understand that I am trying to help you, Mr Holt?' she asked, ramming the point home.

To be truthful I was finding it hard to concentrate on what she was saying. I just kept thinking about this mechanic bloke who checked out a secondhand car I'd been thinking about buying many years back. The car was a red Laser, as I remember, and he reckoned I should pass on it because the clutch was about to go.

'You won't get to the next corner on it,' he warned me. 'A clutch'll cost you more than what you'll pay for the car in the first place.'

I chose to ignore both his expertise and his doomsaying. I bought the car anyway and drove it around for the next six years without it missing a beat, until I rammed it into a factory wall taking a bend too fast in the rain. I wrote the car off and ended up with a broken arm and some stitches in my head. It was the last time I got behind a wheel.

'Mr Holt, do you realise the seriousness of what I am telling you?'

'Oh, I do, doctor. I do. Trust me. You've just convinced me I've had my last drink.'

She smiled at me, not because she believed a word I said, but because she was certain I was bullshitting.

I met up with Curtis the next day and sat with him under the tree sharing a bottle. I'd already decided it would be best not to spoil a nice afternoon with a tale of woe from the doctor. And I didn't want to interrupt the story he was telling about the night his second wife ran off on him and he got down on his knees in the kitchen and prayed to his long dead mother to help him get the love of his life back.

'I had my eyes closed, and I heard this roaring wind, and she came down the chimney over the wood stove, there in the kitchen. She slapped me hard across the face and told me I didn't deserve a woman, good or evil. My own mother used those very words.'

He took a swig from the bottle, wiped it on his sleeve and passed it to me. I held it in my hand and thought long and hard about a drink without taking one.

'How long had she been dead by then?'

'A good twenty years. Maybe thirty.'

'How'd she look after being dead all that time?'

'Just as I expected. Like an angel.'

Curtis and me drank away the afternoon and into the night, trying our best to out-bullshit each other, until he passed out against the tree. I sat staring up at the big black sky until I fell asleep too. I don't remember getting to my feet, or taking off for anywhere, but when I woke the next morning, I saw a hot sun lifting in the sky. I was lying in a paddock in the middle of nowhere. My shoes and socks and shirt were missing and I had bruises and cuts on my arms and feet. I didn't know where I was, how I'd got there, and my pockets were empty as a ghost's coffin. I'd also taken a decent belting. I got to my feet and stumbled across the paddock, trying to stay out of the way of the thistles and thorns.

I came across a road and started walking. It wasn't long before a copper came along. He pulled onto a rise on the side of the bitumen. I was in trouble but was worn out and ready for him to put me away. But he never. He drove me to the local lock-up, dug out a flannelette shirt and some shoes and socks from the lost property box, wrote me a rail pass, even gave me a twenty-dollar note from his own wallet and dropped me at the railway station.

'Your train should be here in around forty minutes. It will get you back into the city.'

I thanked him. And I meant it.

'How'd you end up out here—' he laughed, '—without a car?'

I looked up at the sky and scratched my head. 'Beats me.'

On the train into town, watching the country disappear behind me, I got the shakes real bad. Right then I would have killed for a drink. The train slowed and stopped. Out the window was a forest of empty wooden buildings parked on the side of a hill. There must have been a hundred or more of them – they had made their own little town, without noise or people to bother them. When the train whistle blew and we took off I wished I lived in that town all on my own.

That night I had a nightmare: I was lying in that paddock again in the middle of nowhere, and the sky was full of thunder and scratches of white-hot lightning. I could hear yabbering above the racket. It was two fellas looking down at me and chuckling. One of them was chewing on something. It was my old liver.

I looked down at my belly and saw that my guts had been ripped open.

The nightmare had rattled me and I stayed away from Curtis for a few weeks while I tried drying out. I didn't miss the grog as much as I did his good company. When I'd been on the wagon for record time and felt it was safe to venture out, I tracked him down to his usual spot on the front steps of the old ballroom. Walking down the street to the market, dodging the crowd with their shopping jeeps and baskets and howling kids in prams, I could hear him, wailing out a Hank Williams number, way before I saw him. The guitar playing was as good as ever and the voice surprised me, better than I'd heard it in years.

Between songs Curtis worked the crowd with some of his stories. When he spotted me he waved and served them an old joke of his, for my benefit, I reckon. 'Hey folks, how do you know when you've knocked off a blackfella's jukebox? All the songs are by Charley Pride!'

Later in the afternoon, back under the tree I was sure I'd been kidnapped from, I told him where I'd ended up that other morning and how it had frightened me so much I hadn't had a drink since. I reckoned he wouldn't have a clue about what had happened to me but I asked anyway. 'Do you remember anything about that night, Curtis?'

'Would have been flat-out asleep. Nothing shakes me once I nod off. You could hit me over the head with a house brick. Matter of fact, Sammy, I have been hit over the head with a brick in this park. All I know is, when I come to the next morning, you were nowhere to be seen. Back to your crib, I thought.'

'Well, I weren't. I woke up the other side of shit creek.'

'Maybe you were taken in a spaceship. By them alien fellas.'

'Aliens?'

'Yep. Doris, who I drink with now and then – down by the tram shelter there opposite the hospital – she told me about this time that she was taken by the aliens. They drilled this hole in her neck and put something in there. Some plug or wires.'

'In her neck?'

He offered me the bottle. I pushed it away.

'In her neck. They did her no harm … Old Doris,' he whispered then. 'Couldn't that girl go in the old days. Sweeter than sugar.'

We sat quiet and thought about Doris for a while, until he tapped me on the knee and looked me hard in the eye.

'So that's it for you? No more drink?'

'No more for me, Curtis. I'm staying off it until I can find out how I ended up in that paddock.'

He lifted the bottle up and toasted me.

'Well, here's to your health, Sammy boy. And all the more for me.'

He laughed, drained the bottle, and pointed the neck at me.

'You know the very same thing happened to Hank. More than once.'

'What are you on about, Curtis? You got a fresh story on Hank every week.'

'That's because he comes to me, Sammy. He comes whispering to me in the night sometimes. He'd been playing down south there, in Louisiana, happy as Larry one minute, strumming and yodelling away, a girl lining him up for the night. Hank had been thinking that he'd never felt better in his life. And then, bang, he'd find himself across the border in Tennessee or somewhere a day or two later, in a cheap hotel room, or down an alley, or even backstage at another show, warming to go on stage, with not a clue how he got there.'

'That was caused by the grog?'

'A bit of that. But mostly other stuff. Miss Emma they call it over there.'

'Miss Emma? Some crazy woman get hold of him?'

'No woman. Morphine. Old Hank took it for pain mostly. And a bit of a drift, you'd have to think. It kept him going when he had a show on. But done him in, too. Killed him. The crooked doctors he was seeing made a blue and shot him up with old Emma three times in one day – double, triple-dosed him. He could feel himself dying in the backseat of a car he was riding in. They say he lifted himself right out of his own body before he could be snatched off to hell. He told the devil himself, loud, "You're not pissing on my soul," his exact words.'

'Where'd you hear that?'

'From Hank. He come and told me one night when I was sitting right here.' Curtis shrugged like it was nothing to meet up with the ghost of Hank Williams. He looked across the park at an empty tram drumming by.

'He's still out there some place. That's what happens when you leave your body premature. You is a lost soul.' He nudged me with the bottle one last time. 'You sure you won't share a drink with me?'

'I'm sure of it. I don't want to set you adrift, Curtis. You've been good to me over the years. But I'm done.'

'You really been frightened off, yeah?'

'I have been, near to death.'

'What you going to do, then?'

'Well, I've made a plan for myself. I've got a daughter up north. She's married with a couple of kids I haven't laid eyes on. She give me a number last time I seen her. She was down for the old girl's funeral and she wrote a number on the back of a train ticket for me. I carried it around for more than a year and then I put it to memory because I was afraid I'd lose the piece of paper. You know, Curtis, I've been going over that number in my head most nights since. Scared I might forget it.'

He frowned and nodded his head. 'That's dedication, right there, Sammy. She'd be proud of you for that one.'

'Maybe she would. And maybe not. I was a lousy father to her, you see.'

'I never met a father who wasn't lousy some of the time. Maybe you can make it up to her.'

'That's what I been thinking. Last week I gathered the coins I had sitting on my side table, turned the mattress over, got down on the floor and I came up with enough to call her.'

'You spoke to her already? You should have let me know. That's news, Sammy.'

'Well, no. I got down to the phone box outside the boarding house, full of nerves, I was. I called the number and this woman answered.'

'Your kid?'

'No. Wasn't her. The woman on the line tells me that they moved out, her and the kids and the fella, around a year back. He's some sort of fixer-upper, and he got work at a caravan park just out of the city they were in. Fixing stuff.'

Curtis opened a warm bottle of beer on his back teeth and took a drink. 'You get a new number for her?'

'No. The woman didn't know it. But she gave me an address and the name of the park. The Oasis. Sounds nice, don't you think?'

Curtis closed his eyes like he could see it. 'Sure does. There'll be palm trees there, you can bet. You going to get hold of the number and call her?'

'No. I've made a decision to head up there and see her. Since I've been off the grog, I've saved enough for a one-way ticket. I already bought it.'

'One-way. You sure about that?'

'Don't have a choice. It's all I could afford. You want to come with me? You could make a fair whack up there playing.'

'Not me,' Curtis said. 'This is my place. I got a life-style here.'

I'd bought a ticket on the overnighter, leaving just on dark. I laid out my best pair of pants under the mattress the night before and rinsed out the cotton shirt I'd picked up at St Vinnie's and hung it in the shower. I didn't have a decent pair of shoes and couldn't afford new ones. The best I could come up with was an old pair of boots from Arnold across the hall. I gave them a good clean with a decent dab of cooking oil. He even gave me an old suitcase of his so I could pack some things – spare underwear and socks and a second shirt.

The Promise

I left my room the next morning and walked down by the market on my way to the railway station, hoping to hear Curtis belting out a number one more time. He wasn't around. He'd most likely given the drink a hammering and was sleeping it off. I walked up the hill towards the park, the old suitcase knocking against my leg. I was breathing hard and felt a little tired all of a sudden and took to a bench. In one hand I held the piece of crumpled paper where I'd written down my daughter's address. 'The Oasis,' I mouthed. I had my other hand in my pocket and could feel the train ticket. I watched as this young fella came by, bouncing his football. He walked by me like I was invisible. Not rude or anything. None of us can see what's not there.

AFTER RACHEL

T HERE WAS SOMETHING UP WITH RACHEL, but I couldn't figure out what it was. It had been nagging at me for months. She was forever in a shit mood and got in late at night. She was drinking too. And then she was gone, without a word. The news was broken to me in a Dear John note scribbled on the back of a gas bill she hadn't bothered paying, stuck on the front of the fridge door. I felt betrayed. The least she could have done was tell me to my face, I thought, as I sat at the kitchen table tearing the note into confetti before burning it in an ashtray.

I confronted her in the street, outside her office later that day after work. She tried telling me that it would be best, 'in the long run', not to tell me of her decision in person, as she didn't want to upset me more than she had to.

'Can't you understand? This is best for you. You shouldn't have come here. You're only upsetting yourself. Don't you see?'

'No, I don't fucking see, Rachel. And of course I'm upset. You write, *I'm leaving, take care,* and something about *finding space*. What fucking space?'

'Lower your voice, Stephen. This is my workplace.'

She took her phone out of her bag and checked her messages.

'I have to go. I'm meeting a friend for a drink.'

'What friend?' I grabbed her by the arm. 'Another man, I bet.'

She pulled away from me.

'Don't touch me, Stephen. You're behaving like a lunatic. It's over between us.'

When I tried grabbing her arm again she slapped my face, turned her back on me and walked away.

I mistakenly thought I'd cope okay on my own. It didn't take long before everything fell apart. I couldn't sleep and stopped eating. One of the other attendants at the city car park I worked at, Swooper, noticed that I was chain-smoking and the weight was falling off me. He invited me for a beer after work, but I didn't feel up to it. I hardly knew him and was in no mood to sit down for a beer. He insisted and eventually I gave in.

We washed up after work and headed for a crowded bar across the street. We downed a few beers and threw small talk around before he earnestly rested a hand on my shoulder, like some old mate.

'You look like shit. I've seen this before, you know. The smoking and pacing around and the crash diet. Getting on the speed will fuck you up for life, my friend. Pretty soon your teeth will fall out and you won't be able to shit.'

'Speed? I don't know what you're on about. I've never had a go at the hard gear. Got nothing to do with drugs.'

'Oh.' He threw his head back, suddenly onto me. 'It's a girl. You've been fucked over by your woman.'

He slowly shook his head from side to side.

I downed a half a pot of beer, wiped my mouth and told him about how I'd woken in the morning, two weeks earlier, to Rachel's goodbye note. He nodded knowingly as I spoke, patted me on the knee and said he understood what I was going through. He also claimed he knew a little more.

'I've been through this shit. She wants her space, she wrote? Yeah?'

'That's all she wrote.'

'You know that's a code word, don't you?'

'Code for what?'

'Rooting. I'd bet my last pipe she's been fucking another bloke.'

The thought of Rachel sleeping with another man shocked me.

'No. It's not like that,' I answered, a little surprised that I was so quick to defend her. 'She just needs some time to herself.'

'Whatever,' he said, chuckling to himself. The drink was getting to both of us. 'I'm telling you, a few months down the track you'll run into her on the street, or in a café somewhere, and she'll be with some fella, smooching like a honeymooner. It'll be a bloke you already know. Or the face to go with the name of the fella she couldn't stop talking about when she was having a feed with you, the *lovely* bloke always helping her out with stuff. You'll front her and she'll turn all red and bullshit to you that this thing between them has only just started.'

Swooper looked into the bottom of his glass through one eye and spied a tall dark-haired woman who had just walked into the bar with the other.

'Don't fall for her crap. Nothing worse than a woman making a fool of you.'

He seemed to be talking from experience.

'You got a girlfriend of your own?'

'No, mate. I'm between women at the moment. Too busy playing the field.'

We had a few more beers before I left him mumbling to one of the barmaids. I walked to the train station through the rain. I got off at my stop and it was still pouring. I was wet through and felt miserable knowing that I had nothing to look forward to but an empty house.

Rachel had come back the weekend after she'd left me. She'd called the night before she came and ordered me to stay away from the house until the removal van she'd organised had loaded her stuff and driven away.

'You can trust me, Stephen. I'll only take what's mine.'

Which happened to be almost everything we possessed between us.

I hid behind a tree across from the house and watched as the van was loaded, until Rachel spotted me and marched across the road.

'I asked that you not be here, Stephen. This is harassment.'

I sulked away, embarrassed, and didn't stop walking the streets until I suddenly realised that I'd managed to get myself lost. When I eventually found my way home and put the key in the door I could actually hear the loneliness of the house. As I walked across the bare boards of the hallway – she'd rolled up the fake Persian and taken it with her – my footsteps echoed through the rooms.

There were just a few sticks of furniture left in the house. Although I shouldn't have been, I was shocked. I'd turned up at Rachel's place two years earlier with a backpack stuffed with clothes and a cardboard box full of paperback novels under my arm. Before moving in with Rachel I'd lived in a share house in Richmond. The furniture in that house had belonged to other tenants, not that we had much between us. I'd been a literature student and had dropped out of university in the home stretch, before the end of third year. Others in the house were dropouts too, from one failed venture or another. We didn't have a dollar between us, the house was a crumbling mess, we drank cheap wine out of jam jars and watched TV sitting on upturned stolen milk crates.

Rachel had rescued me from the chaos. We'd met at a seminar organised by the local Job Centre, where Rachel worked as a motivational trainer. While I didn't get much out of the seminar itself, for reasons that are unexplainable now, Rachel and I hit it off. She told me that she had a strong feeling about me; that I had *potential* I was yet to fulfil. I didn't doubt a word she said. I was also desperate to sleep with her, which we did within days of that conversation.

I thought about that first meeting, the great sex we'd started out with — and then the note on the fridge door. As I walked through the house, in tears, I did a quick inventory of what was left. Although the double bed had belonged to her, she left it behind for me, along with a clean fitted sheet, two blankets and a single pillow. Later that night I sat on the bed and hugged the pillow to my chest and pathetically thought how generous she'd been leaving it behind.

In the depths of loneliness over the following weeks, and on the back of my beer-fuelled chat in the bar with Swooper, I would wake in the middle of the night tortured by the thought that since Rachel had left her bed with me, logically she must have moved into a house where a bed was waiting for her. A bed she was most likely sharing with another man and, as Swooper had prophesied, a bed she was rooting in.

She'd also left the kitchen table, two wooden chairs, the fridge she'd stuck the note to, and enough pots and pans and knives and forks to get by on. Not that I'd done any cooking since she'd left, living on black coffee, cigarettes and toast.

There were a few pre-made meals in the freezer, casseroles and soups that had been lovingly prepared by Rachel before being labelled and neatly stacked away. She had explained to me that they'd come in handy on wintry evenings, after we'd got in late from a romantic walk through the park or along the river. We would warm one of the meals on the stove, cuddle up on the couch in front of the TV and watch a romantic movie.

Well, winter was on the doorstep, and the couch and the TV and my girlfriend were gone.

I did pull a frozen block of pea-and-ham soup out

of the freezer one night, but couldn't bring myself to defrost it, let alone eat it. I forgot to put it away and found the container on the bench the next morning sitting in a pool of murky water. I threw the meal in the bin, made myself a cup of coffee and lit another dart. Rachel had weaned me off cigarettes. I hadn't been tempted at all until she left. Conning myself that I hadn't returned to being a serious smoker, I fed my habit by buying the cigarettes loose, in twos and threes, from Ali, at the local milk bar. I'd usually smoke the first of three as we talked out the front of his shop, a second on the walk home, and the precious third and final cigarette sitting with a cup of coffee on the back porch as I looked over the ragged garden. Like the rest of my life, the garden had gone to the pack since Rachel's departure. With the exception of an old olive tree that seemed to thrive on neglect, most of the plants had died.

I was on my way to the milk bar for more cigarettes one Sunday morning when I spotted a rickety wooden ladder leaning against the trunk of an olive tree that grew on the nature strip outside a block of flats at the end of the street. A yellow plastic bucket was sitting on the nature strip, beneath the ladder. I got closer to the tree and noticed a pair of legs, wrapped in thick woollen socks, and a scuffed pair of slippers perched on the top rung of the ladder. I looked higher and saw an old woman picking olives from the tree and throwing them down into the bucket. She looked at me and nodded. I nodded back and walked on.

At the milk bar Ali suggested I increase my supply of cigarettes from three to four, or even five.

'Don't get me wrong. I'm no pusher, man. But if you buy more each time, you will come back not so quick. It is better for you not to run so much. Come again. Back again. You kill yourself like that, man.'

'Maybe, Ali. But I like the walk.'

As I paced the footpath outside the shop, puffing away like a madman, he stood in the doorway complaining about his son's recent trip back to Egypt.

'The bastard, he rings me, every time reverse. Reverse charges. I say "No", but his mother, she is soft. Always, she takes his call. She talks, I pay. Look at me. Fucking idiot.'

A kid brushed by Ali and went into the shop. Although it was a cold morning he was wearing just a singlet, a pair of track pants and no shoes or socks. He was wired no doubt. As we talked Ali occasionally looked over his shoulder, keeping an eye on the kid. He came out a couple of minutes later, empty-handed. As he walked past Ali reached out and grabbed him by the neck.

'The pockets, little thief. Empty the pockets.'

As the kid tried wriggling free a plastic bottle of tomato sauce fell out of his side pocket and bounced on the footpath. Ali released his grip, reached down and picked up the bottle of sauce. The boy ran until he reached the street corner. He turned and screamed out at Ali, 'You fucken wog cunt.'

'I'm not wog,' Ali screamed back, waving the bottle of sauce at the boy. 'I'm Arab.'

He laughed to himself as he studied the bottle of sauce.

'Let me give you no offence, my friend. But this country has nothing. You know how many tomatoes in the bottle? Nothing. Like this country. It's all shit now.'

'No offence taken, Ali. I've got nothing myself.'

I lit another cigarette, said goodbye and walked homeward. Back at the olive tree the old woman was down from the ladder, collecting the loose olives that had missed the bucket. It was almost full. I'd reached my front gate when I stopped and headed back up the street. She looked up at me from her hands and knees.

'I have a tree.' I pointed towards the house. 'In the backyard.'

She stared blankly at me. I wondered if she understood English.

'I have a tree,' I repeated. 'In my backyard there is an olive tree, just like this one. I live at number thirteen.

You can come and have a look if you like? It has olives all over it.'

'Olives?'

'Yep. Lots of big olives.'

She shrugged her shoulders, disinterested, struggled to her feet, picked up the full bucket of olives like it weighed nothing and walked off.

I wasn't back home more than five minutes when there was a knock at the door. I immediately thought of Rachel and hurried to open it. The woman was standing on the doorstep carrying an empty bucket in each hand. An old man dressed in a checked flannel shirt, work pants and muddy boots stood behind her, leaning on the wooden ladder she'd been using in the street. She introduced him as her husband.

'We come to see your tree,' she explained. 'We pick. Olives.'

I opened the side gate and escorted them into the yard. They smiled with delight as they walked around the tree, admiring the abundance of fruit. I went into the kitchen and watched them as they worked together, chatting away in what sounded like Italian, English and, occasionally, something in between. I made myself a coffee, went out into the yard, lit a smoke and watched them more closely. One bucket was already full. They bustled away, shaking the tree like a flock of birds feeding on the fruit.

I didn't want them thinking I was spying on them, so I began tidying up around the yard. I picked up a broken terracotta pot but wasn't sure what to do with it and put it down. I wandered over to the corner of the yard and stopped outside the wooden garage door. In the time that I'd been living at the house with Rachel I'd never been inside the garage. I forced the door open and looked in. The garage was empty except for a piece of furniture sitting in the corner, covered in dust and cobwebs.

It was an ancient record player. My grandmother had had one just the same, when I was a kid. She'd called it a 'three-in-one'. I lifted the veneer lid of the player and saw a record sitting on the turntable. I heard the old woman call me from the yard. She pointed to the overladen buckets.

'We finish olives.'

Her husband, who hadn't spoken a word, had the ladder slung over his shoulder. He bent forward and picked up a bucket in each hand, as she attempted to explain the process of washing and preparing the olives to me, only some of which I understood. She guessed so, and smiled to me as they were leaving by the side gate.

'No matter. I will come back and show. One week. Two weeks. I will have beautiful olives.'

I stood outside the garage and watched as they left

the yard. He was about half a foot taller than his wife. She reached up and rested a hand on his shoulder and they rhythmically waddled from side to side.

Late that night I dragged the old record player into the kitchen with the idea of listening to the radio for company. I dusted off the player with a damp cloth. I plugged it into the wall socket and hesitantly flicked the switch, half expecting an explosion. Nothing happened. For the next hour or so I tried everything I could to get the radio working, pulling wires out of sockets and checking loose connections, with no success.

Mucking around with the wires I accidentally knocked the arm of the record player. The turntable began rotating. I moved the needle across to the vinyl and heard the wonderful crackling notes of the first track on the record. I knew the song well. My parents had once owned the same record.

I dragged one of the kitchen chairs over to the record player, sat down and closely listened to each track on the album. I felt a little sad. Not particularly because of the words or the melody, but with a strong memory of my parents dancing arm-in-arm together in my childhood lounge room. They had been really in love, my mum and dad. When he died of a heart attack, in his fifties, she fell apart and had kept to herself ever since.

★

True to her word, the old woman knocked at my front door a fortnight later. It was a Saturday morning. The jar of olives she was nursing in her arms was enormous. I stepped onto the porch to greet her.

'Your husband? Where is he?'

'Oh, he fell from ladder. Sore back.'

She pantomimed the fall, right down to clutching her back and moaning.

'I'm sorry to hear that.'

She waved away my concerns.

'Better soon.'

I invited her into the house. She looked at me a little suspiciously before following me down the hallway into the near-empty kitchen. Her eyes settled on the record player and chair in the middle of the room.

'The house is empty. You live all alone?'

'Yes. Alone.'

'No good. This makes you sad. I see. You ...' she pointed at me, 'enjoy the olives. They bring peace. They bring luck for you. They bring happy. Eat.'

Before I'd fully comprehended what she'd said she had turned around and marched out of the house. I didn't really know what to do with the jar. I didn't want to offend her and had said nothing about not eating olives. I'd always thought they were a little too *exotic*. I rested my back against the kitchen sink and looked across at the jar. I walked over to it, bent forward and peered through the glass. There must have been hundreds of olives in the jar, along with slivers of red chilli, peppercorns and flakes of sea salt.

I unscrewed the top of the jar, reached in, took out an olive and rested it on my tongue. It tasted warm and fresh. I bit into it. The olive contained many flavours. But most of all it tasted – not like the sea – but *of* the sea. I ate a second olive, quickly followed by a third.

I quit smoking the next morning, and not because I'd made an effort to give up. Each time I took a puff on a cigarette I tasted burnt rubber in my mouth. I also felt sick. Until I ate another olive, which immediately made me feel better. That afternoon I felt motivated to tidy the yard and weed the garden beds. The next day I stocked the fridge with food. I even picked up a comfortable two-seater couch from the secondhand store down the road.

A little over a week later, just as I was fishing around the bottom of the olive jar with my hand, trying to grab hold of the last of the slippery olives, the woman was back on my doorstep with a fresh supply. She smiled and told me I looked a lot healthier.

'More fat,' she said, laughing, as she grabbed her own well-proportioned stomach and jiggled it up and down.

'Yes, more fat,' I answered and lifted my shirt and patted my guts. 'More fat.'

Soon after the woman left there was another knock at the door. Maybe she'd forgotten something? I had not expected to find Rachel on the doorstep. She had changed. Her hair had blonde highlights through it and she'd lost weight.

A little too much weight if you want my opinion.

She was dressed differently too, in tight jeans, black leather boots and a T-shirt with bold sequined letters across the front – LIVE FOR THE MOMENT.

'Hi, Stephen,' she chirped like a busy bird. 'How are you?'

I felt a little awkward and didn't know what to say. I pointed at the T-shirt.

'What's that mean?'

She tugged at the T-shirt.

'It's sort of like a Buddhist thing.'

I was surprised. Rachel had always been more secular than Richard Dawkins.

'Have you become a Buddhist? I'm surprised.'

'No. I said *like* a Buddhist. Silly. It's this cool idea that what's happening now is what matters most. The moment. *Live* for the moment. You know?'

No, I didn't know, but couldn't be bothered saying so.

A car was parked in front of the house, a late-model sedan. Some guy wearing dark glasses was sitting behind the wheel.

'He with you?' I nodded.

I spotted the nervous twitch in her eye.

'Yes. That's Robert from the media department. You must remember him. He's been great to me, helping me get myself together. That's why we're here. Actually. I don't know if you remember it, Stephen, but I had an old record player in the garage. It belonged to my mother.'

I looked at her as vaguely as I could manage and said nothing. She tried prompting me.

'We saw one just like it at a garage sale last weekend. You wouldn't believe what they were asking for it. I'm planning to auction mine on eBay.'

Robert got out of the car, took his sunnies off, rested his hands on the roof of the car and watched me closely. He seemed concerned, like maybe I was going to harm Rachel. I smiled and waved at him. He waved back.

'I'm real sorry, Rachel, but I did a clean out after you left and gave some stuff away. A record player might have been in that lot. I can't be sure. I thought you'd taken everything you wanted with you. I've still got your bed here. Maybe you need that? Or have you found another bed?'

'I just wanted the record player.'

'Well, if it's any help to you, I gave the stuff to the Salvation Army store down on the highway. Maybe they haven't sold it yet?'

'That's okay. It was just an idea.'

She looked me up and down.

'You look well. You've put on some weight.'

'Yeah, a little. I'm good. I eat well.'

'Are you seeing anyone?'

'No. I don't have the time. Work keeps me pretty busy.'

'The car park?'

'Yep. At the car park. It's always busy. You know, moving cars, here and there.'

I could think of nothing more to say to Rachel. She fumbled over a goodbye, walked away and got back into the car alongside Robert. I waited until they'd driven out of the street before closing the front door. I walked back into the kitchen, unscrewed the lid on the fresh jar of olives and scooped a few into a teacup with a large spoon. I took my seat in front of the record player, moved the needle across to the first track of the album and tapped my foot to the beat.

STICKY FINGERS

THE BEATLES HAD BROKEN UP A YEAR AGO and Sparrow had hardly left his bedroom. Once he'd worn out his original copy of *Let It Be*, their final album, he headed straight back to the record shop on Victoria Street and picked up a second copy. On weekends he'd throw open his bedroom window, turn his stereo up full volume and torture us with 'The Long and Winding Road'. Or worse, the title track – more mournful, if that were possible. He had the best sound system of any kid on the estate, a foreign make with a funny name that his old man had lifted from the docks. He'd actually knocked off four of them, but no one on the estate could afford to buy one, even at half price.

While the system produced a great sound, it couldn't save *Let It Be*. Most of the tracks were fit only for a funeral, and are being sung at drunken wakes to this day. Despite our complaints Sparrow wouldn't give the album a rest. Worse still, he skipped the only decent track, 'Get Back', to probe the lyrics of the more depressing songs for some logical explanation as to why the band had so suddenly and completely disintegrated, unconvinced by half the planet's conviction that *it was fucken Yoko*.

He lived with his parents and two older brothers in a first-floor corner flat. His window hung directly above where we wasted our days, catching the sliver of light that cut between two high-rise blocks. We would have been prepared to give up on the precious sun and escape his music if it were not for the fact that our competition marble ring was located on the same spot. When we weren't lying around talking shit to each other, occasionally hurling abuse at Sparrow's open window, or practising the art of blowing smoke rings, we played marbles, practising for the annual City Marbles Championship, the most important date on our sporting and social calendar. The CMC had been set up between the Public Housing Authority and some churchies, to keep kids out of trouble and off the streets. Rather than kick the shit out of each other, teenagers from inner-city public housing estates went to war over the game of marbles.

The tournament was organised across the summer holidays and was run by the Salvation Army one year, and the Catholic Church the following year. Teams of four players, from each of the eight inner city estates, drew each other in a round-robin tournament before the four top-ranking teams played each other in the semis, with the two best teams facing off in the grand final. The team racking up the highest tally of keepsies – the number of marbles won across the early rounds of the tournament – got to play the grand final on their home ring.

Each ring was unique, and having mastery over its peculiar habits provided a genuine advantage. For instance, although you couldn't pick it with the naked eye, the Carlton ring drifted slightly from left to right. Once the pace of a marble had slowed it fell away from the targeted alley or even stopped dead in its tracks. Knowing how a ring played and gaining the valuable experience of regularly practising on it were very different. No home team let an opposition side near their ring until the first set down of a match, so practising away was impossible.

The Collingwood ring was the hardest to play. It had pieces of glass buried just below the surface. While the team had been accused of sabotaging their ring to disadvantage opponents, they'd always claimed that the small shards of glass that popped out of the dirt like a white pointer's fin were actually a 'natural condition' of the ring, as it had previously been used as another ring, for bare-knuckle boxing, where a drink was always had and empty bottles were sometimes smashed, both in celebration and anger.

Dodging the obstacles was not easy. If a speeding alley collided with a jagged tip of glass the marble would miss the target and sometimes ricochet out of the ring altogether, resulting in a 'double-keeps' penalty. A second challenge of the Collingwood ring was that it was located in the middle of the estate, and was surrounded by four hulking towers, home to the most rabid supporters of the competition. When someone wasn't screaming out of their window at you – 'you're going home with a Tom Bowler shoved up your arse' – you were being pelted in the back of the head with a range of missiles as you hunched for a shot.

We had sailed through the early rounds and felt confident. But the day we got the bad news that we'd drawn Collingwood in the semi-final, I came up with the idea that we should steal ourselves some hard-hats from the council yard to protect ourselves against concussion. Bunga Ward, the team captain, overruled me with a direct 'fuck off', and rightly pointed out that the psychological victory that such a sight would provide to the Collingwood team was as good as handing them the match on a plate.

So we went into an important game without protection. And we won. It was possibly our greatest victory, and without doubt Bunga's bravest performance. With the scores locked at the end of four rounds, he went up against the Collingwood captain, Claude 'Fist of Stone' McVicar, in a sudden-death game of chasey round the ring. With McVicar winning the lag and ordering Bunga to shoot, he fucked up the follow on and kissed Bunga's alley with a breath of air as his taw skidded by and came to a halt on the far side of the ring.

Bunga had to land just one punch and it was over. I ground my teeth down as I watched him hunching for the shot. He crouched like a cat and shut his bad eye that had been clipped by a stray slug from an air rifle when he was about six years old. He slipped his left hand down his pants and tugged at the end of his dick as he concentrated on the shot. It was a good sign. I'd been playing marbles with him since primary school and whenever he gave his foreskin a working over he was on his game. It was like conjuring the magical genie out of the lamp. I had no doubt he'd make the important shot.

Until a homemade dart, thrown from a window high above the ring, speared him in the side of his head. Most any other kid would have collapsed. But not Bunga. He gave the foreskin a final rub and released the marble from his knuckle like a cannon ball. It slammed into McVicar's alley and catapulted it from the ring.

After the game McVicar shook hands with Bunga, which was customary.

'Sorry about the dart, Bung. Someone upstairs must have had a few dollars on the game. I hope this doesn't cause bad blood between us.'

Bunga rubbed his wound and said there were no hard feelings and Claude wished us well against the Kensington team in the grand final the following week.

'I hope you kick their arse all the way back to the western suburbs. Shit. They're not even a city team. We played them out there in the round robin, and I needed a torch and a fucken map to get the boys home for tea.'

Luckily, we were playing 'The Ken' at home, where we'd thrashed them four weeks earlier in the round robin. Over the years our ring had been beaten to hardened clay. It was the fastest surface in the competition and on a warm day played like polished glass. Any player unfamiliar with its speed found it hard to play.

Bunga came up with the idea to add to our advantage by driving the opposition team crazy: he instructed me to have Sparrow ready with the miserable sighs of Paul McCartney on the morning of the match.

'You tell him I want that sad stuff up full blast as soon as we hit the ring.'

'You sure? It might fuck us instead. You hate the shit.'

'But we've got these,' he said, and pulled a packet of

industrial earplugs out of his pockets. 'We'll put these in as soon as the music starts.'

'You got enough for all of us?'

'More than enough. My old man brings them home from the forge and puts them in of a night so he doesn't have to listen to my mum talking.'

'That must piss her off.'

'Nah. She stopped talking to him a long time back, but he doesn't know that because he wears the earplugs. He's had to learn to lip-read off the TV.'

The day after the Collingwood win, my dad loaned us a tarp off his truck so we could cover the ring when we weren't practising on it. Any rain on the clay would slow it up. I caught Sparrow on his way home from school the next afternoon, just as he was climbing the stairs to his flat. When I told him Bunga wanted him to crank up his stereo on the day of the match, with the bad side of the Beatles album, and be sure his windows were open, he was surprised.

'Are you sure that's what he wants? I don't want to get into trouble and my mum's sick of him yelling out, "I'm gonna cut your fucken power if you don't turn it down, Sparrow."'

'It's what we all want. You can help us win. I'm here on his say-so, so don't worry.'

He was unconvinced.

'Maybe he'd like some Hendrix or Cream? My brother Dom's got all their stuff. He's into guitar solos. I could borrow some of his albums.'

'He's got some Hendrix? Shit. I've never heard any *Hey Joe, where you goin' with that gun in your hand?* coming out of your window.'

He tapped the side of his head.

'He wears headphones and it's sending him deaf. I thought he must've done it last year when he let off that string of tom-thumbs in his own face on Guy Fawkes Night. My mum took him to the doc and he says it's the loud music that's fucked him up.'

'Don't worry about Hendrix or your brother, Sparrow. We need you to concentrate. Stick with the Beatles. Okay?'

'Okay,' he shrugged. 'If it's what you want.'

The CMC grand final was timed to coincide with the last weekend of the school holidays. We spent most of the week leading up to it at the ring, practising pressure shots, exercising our shooting thumbs and listening to motivational rants delivered by Bunga. He insisted we take a tram into the city and watch a re-run of *Ben Hur* that was showing at the Metro on Bourke Street. I came out of the film knowing something more about chariot races and a little about the Bible, but nothing revealing about the game of marbles.

The two other members of our team were Bung's younger brother, Fatman, a very good player for his age, who'd been described in the *Richmond Gazette* as a 'sporting prodigy', and Scratch, a Scottish kid who'd only been in the country for six months. He wasn't too popular, seeing as he was always scratching at his arse-hole, a habit that didn't seem to bring him luck, good or bad. But his more hygienic hand was steady as a rock and he had a beautiful eye for splitting a pair of alleys when the pressure was on.

Two days out from the big day, disaster struck the team. We were at practice and I was clearing the ring of marbles. I looked across at Bunga. He was working on his shooting thumb with a sheet of sandpaper. He'd turned a rich-red colour and the sweat was pouring off him.

'Hey, Bung? You okay?'

He kept rubbing away at the thumb.

''Course I am.'

'You need a drink of water or something? You look like you're cooking.'

'Nope. Don't need water. Water's bad for you.'

Before finishing up that night, we swept the ring, covered it with the tarp and planned to meet early the next day. When I showed up in the morning Scratch was already there, digging away at his bum with one hand and eating a cold untoasted crumpet with the other. We nodded and grunted to each other. I'd tried actually talking to Scratch a few times but couldn't understand a word he said except for 'Foke', which hadn't got us all that far.

Fatman sidled over to the ring a full half hour later. He sat down on a turned-up rubbish bin and stared at the ring. I threw a marble at him to get his attention.

'Wake up, Fatty. Where's Bung? He told me not to be late.'

He huffed and puffed and shifted his feet around in the dirt.

'He's not coming.'

'What do you mean, not coming? This is the last practice before the game.'

'There's not going to be any game,' he almost cried.

'You're talking shit.'

'Last night,' he blurted out, 'he woke up in the night and started heaving onto the bedspread and crying about this pain in his head. The old man took his temperature with his old army thermometer and it was over a hundred or something, so he put him in the back of the car and drove him to St Vincent's. He's got a killer infection or something. When Dad come home just then I heard him whispering about some operation to my mum. I think he might die.'

'We ner foked now,' Scratch howled.

'Exactly,' I agreed.

There was no more news about Bunga that day or night. The next morning Fatman knocked at my door and told me that he was going to the hospital to visit his brother and that I could come if I liked.

'Is he better then?'

'I dunno. My old man just banged on our bedroom door and told me to stop being a lazy cunt and go visit him in hospital to cheer him up. Maybe he's better. Or ...' Fatman snorted and swallowed his own snot, 'or maybe like I said yesterday, he's dying or something.'

'He wouldn't be dying, or your father would be at the hospital with him, wouldn't he?'

'Suppose so. But it's payday and he always has a drink and a bet.'

My mother said I could have some tram money to go and visit him. I decided to walk instead and used some of the money to buy him a bag of mixed lollies and a *Phantom* comic. Fatman and Scratch walked with me. They pooled their coin and bought a small packet of Viscount cigarettes. We had a smoke out front of the hospital, ate a couple of lollies each from the bag and caught the lift to the top floor.

I spotted Bunga sitting up in bed at the end of a long narrow ward. He had a great view of all the building cranes across the city. Most of the other patients in the ward were old men who didn't move a lot. He seemed well enough and smiled and waved at us as we walked between the rows of beds. Wearing a new pair of striped pyjamas he looked like a little kid again. I gave him the lollies and the comic and he opened the top drawer of a cupboard next to the bed, pulled out a ham–and–pickle sandwich and offered it to me.

'Get stuck into that. The old fella next to me can't eat a thing. They cut part of his tongue out because of some cancer. He's ate nothing, but they keep bringing him stuff.'

I unwrapped the sandwich and took a bite. It was real ham, not the fake stuff you get in a tin.

'You don't look sick, Bung. Fatman here said you were about to drop dead.'

'I didn't say he'd dropped dead,' Fatty defended himself. 'I said he might be dying. It's not the same thing, idiot.'

'Well, I'm not dying. I had to have this infection cut out and they've given me pills to help me get better.'

'Cut out? Where'd they cut the infection from?' Fatman asked. 'I asked Mum what was going on. She wouldn't tell me. "Ask your father," she said.'

'I'll show you. Take a look at this.'

He pushed the blanket to the bottom of the bed, undid the ties on his pyjama pants and pulled them down to his knees. The four of us were staring at the knob of his dick. It was bloodied and bruised and bandaged in yellow-stained gauze.

'Shit. What happened?' I asked.

'The foreskin bit got all infected. The doctor said I'd gotten germs in it because I've been playing with it too much, so they had to snip it off.'

'Foke,' Scratch whispered.

My father appealed to the Victorian Junior Marbles Board on our behalf and the grand final was put back two weeks. It was another week before Bunga could move around on his own and piss without too much pain. By early in the week before the final he was just about back to his old self, giving us orders down at the marbles ring. We were back in full training a couple of days later.

On the morning of the match Bunga reminded me to call up to Sparrow's flat and organise the music. I had to knock at his door three times before somebody answered. His mother said he wasn't home.

'Where's he at then? Sparrow's in charge of playing the music for the marbles final.'

She lifted her bottom lip and sneered at me.

'Play his music? So you cheeky bastards can give him hell again? You and your cross-eyed mate.'

Bunga wasn't cross-eyed. He had a lazy eye. Just one.

'We're not going to abuse him. We want him to put some songs on. I already asked him and he said he'd do it.'

'Well, he can't do it, because he's not here.'

She tried closing the front door on me.

'Where's he gone?'

'Where would you think? To the record shop. I'm sure he's got a bed there.'

'When he gets back can you ask him to put the Beatles on? Loud.'

'I'll be out doing the shopping. You see him, ask him yourself.'

Back at the ring the team was warming up.

'You got him organised?' Bunga growled.

'Yep,' I lied. He was always grumpy before a big match. I didn't want him losing concentration worrying over where Sparrow might be.

By the time the Kensington team arrived, in a Salvation Army minibus, a large crowd had gathered, including teams from the other estates. A few of the dads had turned up, but kept their distance from the ring, enjoying a smoke and an early beer under a scraggy gum tree across from the ring.

Before each match the regulations governing the game of marbles were read aloud by a Salvation Army Major. Although he was forever encouraging us to call him Major Bob, most kids knew him as Dr No. He called the event to attention.

'There shall be *No* swearing – *No* raucous barracking – *No* spitting on or near the ring – *No* walking through the ring – *No* coaching from the sidelines – *No* oversized or overweight marbles – *No* unacceptable attire to be worn by team members.'

We won the opening lag, with Bunga lobbing his alley only a freckle short of the line. We would be shooting first up. Bunga handed us our earplugs and looked up at Sparrow's closed window.

'Is he ready with the music?'

'Should be,' I lied again. 'His mum said he'd be ready.'

'His mum? She hates me. You were left in charge of this.'

'Don't worry, he'll be there.'

I eyeballed three of the Ken team across the ring, all of them scabby-faced runts.

'Don't worry, Bung. They look beaten before the start. One of them's a pinhead.'

We decided to run with our standard order. Fatman would lead off, followed by me, then Scratch, and finally Bunga, to bring home the win.

Fatman got us off to a poor start. He missed shots he'd usually nail blindfolded; such is the pressure of a grand final. He trailed by three with only two alleys left in the ring on the second-last pair. He got lucky when his opponent over-hunched on the shot, lost his balance and fell into the ring – an automatic two marble penalty – leaving Fatman a marble down but controlling the play. He was about to shoot when Bunga noticed his hand shaking and a trickle of sweat running down the side of his face.

He called time-out and ordered Scratch to go fetch Fatman some water.

'Fatty, you need to take the pair with one shot. But forget about this being the final. It's just another game and you're gonna win it.'

Fatty hadn't heard a word he'd said, and pulled his ear plugs out.

Scratch handed him a milk bottle full of water. He took a long gulp. Bunga repeated his order.

'But you've been saying all along at training that if I lost my match you'd skin me alive and cook me in a pot.'

'Yeah, well, I might do that even if it was just another game. Do your job and take out the pair.'

Fatman did as Bunga asked. His taw clipped the first alley, which cannoned into the second, knocking both marbles out of the ring. Game over.

Bunga ordered me to warm up. He started barking orders at Scratch.

'Scratch, run upstairs and see if Sparrow's ready. We need the Beatles on.'

He grabbed hold of my shooting thumb and loosened it for me.

'You seen their number four yet? They can't back up with a player who's already shot, can they? I'm going to speak to Dr No.'

I looked across the ring at the Ken team. The three runts were busy talking to a couple of girls. One of the girls lit a cigarette. They shared a puff. They were as good-looking as the boys were ugly. I couldn't take my eyes off one of them. She was wearing a Harlem Globetrotters singlet and cut-down jeans. She had long, long legs and beautiful tanned skin that glowed like honey.

'Hey, Bung. What do you think of her?'

'Concentrate on the game, dickhead.'

But I couldn't concentrate. Each time I hunched for a shot the golden-skinned girl positioned herself across the ring from me. She didn't seem to mind me staring at her. She might have smiled at me, although I couldn't be sure. By the time I got my game on track it was all over. I'd been slaughtered, six marbles down and out. Luckily Scratch wasn't distracted by her and played beautifully. He had the best long shot in the competition and didn't disappoint, wiping the ring with the third of the runt brothers. We were two–one up, with our best player still to come and no sign of the Ken number four.

When Dr No called for the 'final player of each team to present themselves at the line' Bunga raised his arms above his head like a champion boxer, thinking it was all over. Cheering broke out across the crowd. Dr No took a small brass bell and stopwatch from his side pocket, rang the bell and announced a 'two-minute warning'. If the Ken number four didn't step forward before the bell sounded a second time the match was all ours.

With just seconds left on the Major's stopwatch the golden-brown girl stepped up to the line and offered Bunga her hand. He screwed his nose up at her.

'What do you think you're doing? Only registered players are allowed to come to the lag line. Piss off back to your girlfriend.'

'Piss off yourself, fuck-face. I am the player.'

'You can't be the player. You're a girl.'

'Yeah. I'm a girl. Not that you'd know. And I'm the player, so let's get on with it.'

'This is bullshit.'

He called on Dr No for a ruling.

'Hey, Doc. They must be stalling for time or something. Tell her she can't play.'

An argument broke out between the teams and some in the crowd as Dr No went to the rulebook, with Bunga looking over his shoulder. Fatman pulled him aside.

'Who cares that they've fronted with a girl? Kick her arse and it's over.'

Bunga focused his good eye on Fatman.

'Are you fucken kidding me? I'm not playing a girl. 'Course, I'll beat her. So what? Any of us could beat her. I'll cop shit over this for years.'

Dr No went through the book twice before announcing to the crowd that there was 'no rule or sub-clause governing the sex of a player'.

He ordered both players to the line.

I've thought about what happened next many times. Sometimes I almost convince myself that the whole day was a dream; there was never any beautiful girl with golden-brown legs; and there was no grand final held at our ring. Whenever I find myself overcome with doubt I'll ask Fatman or Scratch if they remember the final game of the CMC that year the same as I do. They do, although Fatty remembers her legs being even longer and browner and more golden. For a reason that escapes me, Scratch claims not to recall her legs at all. But he is sure that she was able to play equally well on both sides of her body, and could shoot left- and right-handed, a rare skill in competition marbles.

With Bunga continuing to complain to Dr No, the girl won the lag and chose to shoot first. She catwalked around the ring, picking off alleys with ease, for the following ten minutes. Those who weren't fixated on the game were hypnotised by her legs, including Dr No, who was wiping his brow with a damp hankie. After taking out four alleys in a row, the crowd was cheering for her. By the time she'd knocked out eight marbles people were going crazy. When she was down to the last alley standing, a black eye, which according to marbles folklore was a curse upon the shooter, the crowd was silent.

In possibly an act of desperation, or an involuntary nervous twitch, Bunga dug a hand into his jeans pocket – the one with the hole in it – and reached for his lucky foreskin. But of course, there was no foreskin to be found. All he could do was revert to religion and began praying for a miracle, by way of a Hail Mary, as the girl hunched on the far side of the ring.

I forgot all about Bunga and the game that was at stake. I smiled at her and peeked a look at her thighs as they caught the sun. She winked at me and played her kill shot. The taw slammed into the black eye with so much power the marble split in two. I'm sure I saw smoke rising from the ring. The Ken team and their supporters went wild and the runts threw their arms around her. One of them tried squeezing her tits.

According to the rules, Bunga was entitled to shoot at a second set-up. If he could miraculously match her lockout, a sudden-death shoot-out would decide the winner. But he was already beaten and he knew it. He dropped his favourite marble in the dirt without playing a shot and walked away from the ring without looking back. Fatman and Scratch ran after him, but I disloyally hung around for the presentation, hoping to talk to the girl. The winner's trophy was awarded and the team were hurried back onto their bus before a fight broke out; another tradition of the CMC tournament.

When the bus was about to leave I walked over and knocked at the window.

'Hey, will you be playing marbles again next year?'

'I don't reckon,' she shrugged. 'This is boring. Maybe you'd like to play a different game,' she laughed, as the bus took off.

I chased it along the street, yelling at her, 'What game? What game?' until the bus had disappeared around the corner at the end of the street.

The four of us sat in silence at the ring for the afternoon. Scratch tried offering words of support but Bunga would have needed an interpreter out of a Glasgow slum to make sense of what he'd said. Just before the sun went down Sparrow came walking across the grass towards us. He was carrying a brown paper bag from the record shop.

'How'd the grand final end up, Bunga? You win?'

'Get fucked, Sparrow.'

Sparrow had bought himself a new record. He'd want to tell us all about it, and wouldn't be put off by Bunga's rudeness.

'Do any of you want to see the new album I bought?'

'Get well and truly fucked,' Bunga screamed.

Sparrow ignored him and took the record from the bag. A photograph filled the album cover, showing some bloke's crotch in a pair of Levi's jeans.

'Another Beatles album?' I asked. 'I thought they were rooted.'

'It's not the Beatles. I think it's time to move on.'

'You're right it is,' Bunga yelled. 'You should start now. I told you, fuck off.'

'You might be cured, Sparrow,' I laughed. 'Who is it?'

'The Rolling Stones. Wait here and I'll go upstairs and play it. Let me know what you think.'

A couple of minutes later his bedroom window went up. The opening guitar riff hit me like a thunderbolt. By halfway through the track even Bunga was tapping his foot to the beat, and when the song was over he was smiling wide enough to swallow his ears.

THE PROMISE

CAROL HAD WARNED ME OFTEN enough that she was going to leave, so when I got home late from playing cards and a big drink at Winston's and found her gone I wasn't surprised. She'd taken off to her folks' place, dragging the boys with her. She'd done the same three times in the past year. I woke up the next morning with a sore head expecting she'd be back by the end of the day, but she didn't turn up.

It was another two weeks before she'd come to the phone when I called her at the farm. She told me that she wouldn't be home again unless I showed *commitment*. Just for a start she wanted me signed up for a rehab program.

'Is that all I need to do, honey?'

'Is that all? How many times have you promised, Luke, and done nothing?'

'This will be different, Carol. This house is like a

117

morgue without you and the boys here. This is a real promise.'

I could hear her mother's whining voice coaching her in the background.

'You sign up for a program before I come back. And I want to see proof. One of them authority notices the government's put out. All right?'

I had a chuckle after I put the phone down. Rory Collins, a mechanic at the garage on the main street, an amiable man I drank with from time to time, had a brother-in-law who'd worked as a drug-and-alcohol counsellor with the City before he'd fallen off the wagon himself. He'd gotten the sack from his job, having gone near blind on homemade firewater he'd cooked up in his backyard. On his way out of the counselling service he'd lifted a fat pad of pledge authorities and had been selling them for twenty bucks apiece ever since.

The biggest business in town was grog. Always had been. Closely followed by the church, and after that, since the government crackdown, came drug-and-alcohol counselling. None of the charities in town would give a man as much as a cup of tea without a signed authority note. The dole office was likely to cut off your cheque if you were an identified pisshead and not in a program. The counsellors ran the show, so they benefited most from the graft – cash, grog or girls. Sometimes the unholy trinity, if they were particularly greedy.

Three days after the phone call and Carol's demand, I was ready to head over to the in-laws' with a signed authority in my pocket. I'd forged the signature myself.

I'd picked up a suit jacket at the Salvation Army, had a shave and spit-polished my only pair of leather shoes. I'd even thought about a haircut, but decided against it, calculating that the twelve dollars would be better spent on a six-pack of Rebel Yell. I settled for some ancient hair oil I found in the back of the medicine cupboard in the bathroom before heading off.

The oil had belonged to my grandfather, Abraham, a mission black who'd found God as a young man and who'd known the Bible, Old Testament and New, word for word. He'd bought our two-room weatherboard, on a low rise in the middle of town, with the money he'd earned over twenty backbreaking years as a ditch worker for the Water Board. Abe had a plan to set up his own church in the back room of the house, but as he got older and hunched over, the idea slipped away from him. Even then he never stopped reading his Bible, and slept with it under his pillow.

He had taken good care of me after my mother ran off with some whitefella. My father had been white, too, a cattle worker passing through town heading west for a run; he'd stayed long enough to woo my mother back to his hotel room one night and send her home pregnant. When her belly got too big to hide under a dress, Abraham prayed for her and explained that she could stay in the house as long as she promised to get down on her hands and knees every night and pray with him. Dulcie, my mother, didn't have much choice. Back in those days, if a pregnant black girl didn't have a safe roof over her head and someone decent to speak for her, she'd have the baby whipped from her breast soon after it was born. She knew that Abraham's word was the Gospel itself, and kept her promise until I started crawling around on the floor and making demands of her that she wasn't interested in meeting. She got the wanders and eventually travelled far enough from us that she didn't bother finding her way home.

For a while I reckoned my father must have been an albino, because I was the fairest-skinned blackfella in the history of the town and could have easily passed for white. Abraham showed no prejudice towards me and tried steering me on the right path, but as soon as I was old enough I drifted out to the lake, to the ruins of the Christian mission, and quickly learned to love the drink and the smell of a girl's skin after it had been dipped in water and wine.

Abraham left the house to me after his death. It wasn't much of a prize, but it was enough to impress Carol, a farmer's daughter who worked at the bank in town and knew all about the value of private property.

'It's a start,' she said softly, when she first saw the place, as rundown as it was.

I met her during one of my brief periods of sobriety, a time when I went around town in a clean white shirt and talked about reviving Abraham's dream of a church of his own. I'd even dressed the story up for Carol, in an effort to get her into his old brass bed – I told her I'd sworn to him, on his deathbed, that I would build his church and fill it with believers.

'And what did he say?' she'd pleaded, tears in her eyes, as we sat in the only tearoom in town, drinking Earl Grey out of flowery cups.

'Well,' I said, as I took a long gulp of the tea and stalled for an answer, 'he looked up at me with that wrinkled old face of his, and even though he was in a mess of pain he said to me, "I know you can do it, Luke. You're a strong boy. The Lord will be pleased, and I'll rest easy."'

Carol leaned across the table and rested her head against my chest. I put my arms around her and pressed her body into mine. She smelled so clean and soapy and pure, I was sure we'd be happy together.

The days of scandal, of a white girl marrying a half-caste, weren't quite over. The town whispers followed us wherever we went. But when I met Carol's parents in Abraham's dusted-off black suit and told them of my plans for a church, they seemed satisfied.

'Land,' her mother gushed to her husband, almost in disbelief. 'He has *land*.' Meanwhile the old man looked over at Carol and thought, to my reckoning, that she was a bit of a wallflower and this might be his best chance of marrying her off. He took her by the hand and told her he was happy for us.

They lived far enough out of town to have no direct experience of my reputation, and never made inquiries, which would have turned up trouble for me. To this day I think that maybe they didn't want to know.

I did love Carol, then and now. But not as much as I loved the grog and the good company of them old boys. I loved the stories they told about the old days, when there was just a handful of whitefellas on the horizon. I also loved the town girls who drifted out to the lake to lie by the water of a night and look up at the stars. After a time, of course, the boys died away, and the girls grew into women with a tribe of kids of their own and an old man for each of them. If one of them fellas caught his wife out at the lake he'd kick her arse all the way back to town and throttle any man caught jazzing with her.

★

Before leaving the house for the farm I downed my first
can of Rebel Yell at the kitchen sink and threw another
couple onto the passenger seat of the old Datsun, then
set out to lay my claim on Carol and the boys. Along
the way I stopped at the cemetery out of town, sat on
a gravestone, drank another can and plucked a bunch
of flowers from the grave to present to Carol as a peace
offering. I shook the dust off them and sat them on the
seat with the last of the grog.

A couple of minutes' drive away from the turn-off
into the farmhouse I pulled over to the side of the road,
under an old peppercorn tree. I hopped out and took a
piss and then sat under the tree and sipped at the third
can of bourbon and cola while I enjoyed the peace and
quiet of the afternoon. When I'd finished I shook the
last dregs out of the can, crushed it in my hand and
threw it way off into the bushes. I dug into my jacket
pocket and pulled out the half pack of XXX mints I'd
planted there earlier, and then went to the side-view
mirror to look at my face. I checked my bloodshot eyes
and sucked and crunched on those mints and then I spit
in my hands and tucked my wild head of curls behind
my ears. I winked at myself in the mirror, pleased that
I'd scrubbed up okay, all things considered.

My head didn't feel too good. In the car I rested
my chin on the steering wheel and focused as best I
could to keep to my side of the road. I took the turn

123

into the in-laws' long driveway a little too fast and managed to clean up the mailbox, which shattered into kindling. I held my hand down on the car horn so the boys would hear me and come running to see their dad. But they didn't come running at all. I pulled up out front of the house, with its long wide verandah and boxes of pretty flowers. There was no sign at all of Carol or the boys. Just Ma and Pa, old Martha and Ted, waiting to greet me.

I fell out of the car, landed on my hands and knees in the dust, and looked up at them.

'Heya, Teddy,' I said. 'Can you tell Carol I'm here? To pick her up, and the boys. She got her things packed?'

Ted was wearing his bib-and-brace farmer's overalls and a straw farmer's hat. He hadn't done any fieldwork for as long as I could remember; he hired in black-fellas on the cheap to do the slog while he sat on the phone nattering to his big city stockbroker. Martha was wearing one of her pretty floral dresses and a ton of make-up. She never got out of bed of a morning without doing her face. Probably wouldn't recognise her if I came across her sleepwalking. They were full of disgust, both of them.

'She doesn't want to see you,' Martha said, laughing and crying hysterically all at the same time. 'She's had enough, Luke. Carol wants a divorce.'

Ted shifted awkwardly on the balls of his feet, maybe thinking that Martha had played her trump card a little early. I dusted myself off and pulled the forged authority from my jacket pocket.

'She won't need any divorce,' I said, waving the slip of paper in their faces. 'I signed up for a program, just like she asked me to. I'm off the grog. And I'm staying off it.' I tried handing Ted the slip of paper, but he wouldn't take it. 'You ask her to come out here and talk to me right now,' I went on. 'She's my wife, they're my children, and I'm taking them home.'

Martha tut-tutted and shook her head, and silent Ted went red in the face with embarrassment. My story was so full of bullshit I think he felt sorry for me. I heard the screen door slam on the verandah.

'You've got no right being here, Luke.'

It was Carol. She marched past her parents and down off the porch so we were standing toe-to-toe.

'I don't want you upsetting the boys. Like Mum says, I'm not coming back. It's over.'

I pushed the authority slip into her face.

'You told me, on the phone, if I went on a program you'd give me another chance. Well, I did. Read it, Carol. Read it. I am clean and working hard on this. I love you, Carol.'

She snatched the piece of paper out of my hand, screwed it into a ball and threw it to the ground.

'Clean! You've never been clean, Luke. You're dirty, dirty, dirty! You and all your kind. Look at you. You're drunk now! I can smell it all over you. I got a call from Jenny Oakes, from the bank – she told me you were in there yesterday morning cashing a cheque, and by noon, when she was out getting her lunch, you were sitting up in the front bar of The Royal, half drunk. You're not in any program.' She pointed along the drive. 'Leave here now. You shouldn't have driven out here as it was. That car's got no registration and you've got no licence to drive it. I hope the police get hold of you and lock you up.'

I took a step back. My legs started shaking. Ted walked over and put a hand on my shoulder.

'Please, Luke,' he said. 'We don't want any trouble here. I'll drive you back into town, if you like.'

Martha rested her arms across her flat breasts and pulled a face. 'Have you anything to say to my daughter, Luke? Maybe an apology?'

'Yeah, I've got something to say, Martha. To Carol, and to all of you.'

I did have plenty to say. I just couldn't remember what it was right then. I shook my head, trying to loosen the thought, but it wouldn't come. If I'd had a dollar for every time Carol had threatened to leave, I'd be the richest blackfella in the country – richer even than those boys working on the oilrigs off the coast up north. But this time I could feel the pain deep in my gut because I knew there'd be no getting her back.

I got into the car, fumbled with the keys until I could find the ignition and drove off.

At home I went through the medicine cupboard again and grabbed hold of all the pills I could find. Sleeping tablets, antidepressants, painkillers, a few vitamins and even some cough drops. I shoved them all in my gob, stuck my head under the tap and drank until I'd swallowed the lot. I was desperate for another drink, but couldn't remember where I'd dropped the last cans of Rebel Yell. Rifling through the refrigerator I found a lonely can of beer at the bottom of the empty vegetable tray. I drank it, stuck my head in the pantry, came out with half a bottle of vanilla essence and downed that as well.

Abraham had kept a shotgun all his life. He'd never fired it, as far as I knew, but he liked to keep hold of it, claiming that one day he might be called upon to 'protect the righteous from the sinners, black, white and brindle'. The gun wasn't hard to find; I crawled under his old double bed, the wedding bed, and searched around until I found the loose floorboard, then fished around some more until I felt the cold steel of the barrel. I knew the gun was loaded without having to cock it. 'Have it on the ready,' Abe had instructed me. The breech had held a .12–gauge birdshot cartridge for as long as I could remember.

I was ready to shoot myself right there in the house, but thinking about the mess it would make, about Carol or somebody else finding me with half my head caked to the ceiling, I stood up and walked onto the front verandah. It had begun to rain. I looked out across the hills behind the town, at a stand of trees in the distance, and then back at the lonely house. I knew then that I would never be coming back and decided I couldn't abandon it this way.

I went around back to the shed and threw some tools, old tins and chaff bags around until I found the half can of petrol I kept for the mower. I walked slowly through the house, from room to room, dousing each of them. The petrol trailed me along the passageway, out onto the verandah to the front yard. I struck a match and the flame chased the petrol back into the house. The place was fully alight in less than a minute, the dry old boards cracking with pain and weeping off the last traces of paint Abraham had put to them years back. I could hear the windows exploding with rage as I turned away from the flames and started up the car.

Driving out of town I held the gun between my knees with the barrel scratching at my throat. If it had gone off then and there I'd have died a reasonably happy man. Would've saved me from testing my courage. Between the pelting rain, a dirty windshield, fucked wiper blades, and the pills and grog, I was driving on the last prayer I had. The car wobbled and weaved across the highway, by some miracle dodging trucks and trees and some livestock. Cows, mostly. I don't know if it was one of them I hit, or one of those ghost trees they talk about round here that appear out of nowhere, but the last thing I remember was head-butting the windshield.

When I woke my mouth was full of dirt and blood. I lifted my head and tried opening my eyes; I could see out of one, but the other was clamped shut. I'd been thrown from the car and was lying in a muddy ditch, the Datsun to the side of me, its windshield caved in, the door slung open and steam pouring from the bonnet. Something warm and sticky oozed from the corner of my bad eye, down my cheek. I tried getting to my feet and fell down again, up to my arse in murky water.

I swallowed a few breaths and crawled over to the shotgun lying in the mud a few feet from me. I used it to haul myself up and get out of the ditch, onto the side of the red-dirt road. The car was fucked and wouldn't be going anywhere. All my life I'd been walking the roads skirting the town – I thought I knew all of them. I didn't have a clue where I was. There was nobody around and no buildings to identify with, save a rundown hay shed.

It had stopped raining, but a death-rattle wind cut through to my skin. I started to walk, which wasn't easy, as I was missing a shoe and had done an injury to my right foot. I could still get it over and done with and shoot myself, of course, but suddenly it didn't seem such a smart idea. This would be a lonely place to die. The car crash had shaken me up enough to make me know I was a coward.

I dragged myself along the road and eventually rounded a bend and came to a crossroad. There were no signs to tell me which way was which. Heading straight on seemed as good a choice as any, so I walked on, hauling my bad foot with me.

After a while I spotted a white wooden cross and the pitched roof of a church through some trees in the distance. I got closer and could see that it was a small wooden building, resting on a bank above a dry riverbed off the road. The arched front door was open. I made for it.

The doorway was draped with a deep-red velvet curtain. I pulled it to one side and went in. The light was low and it was hard to see. There were people on either side of the room, some sitting behind fold-up tables with colourful card decks laid out, others, mostly old girls, sitting opposite empty chairs with heads bowed and eyes closed, in front of flickering candles, which gave the women a creepy look. A few looked up at me as I walked in, splattered in mud and blood and carrying the shotgun. None of them seemed disturbed by the intrusion. They went back to what they were doing, which was most likely some form of meditation.

A woman at one of the tables wouldn't take her eyes off me. She was older, but beautiful nonetheless, with thick dark curls and the fullest lips I'd ever seen. I wanted desperately to kiss her. She began laying out her cards. I was drawn across the room to her.

'You've had a troubled day, son,' she said, when I reached her. 'Would you like to put that gun down and rest your leg on this stool here?'

I propped my weight on the shotgun and looked around the room. 'What's this place?' I asked.

'We are the Church of Spiritual Healing,' she said, and smiled; her voice was sweeter than I thought could have been possible. She was a songbird. 'We are here to heal the wounded souls that roam.'

'Really? How long you been round here? I know every inch of this country. It don't look it, but the church must be new?'

She turned another card and laid it on the table. Her smile disappeared. She studied the card and then my face.

'No. We have always been here. For all time. Please sit.'

I rested the gun against the side of the chair and took the weight off my bad leg. She tapped softly on the table with her fingertips.

'Is there something you would like to tell me?'

I looked across the table, into her sparkling green eyes. She must have been fifteen or twenty years my senior, but I did want to say something; I wanted to tell her that she was the most beautiful creature I'd ever seen.

'My wife, she's taken off on me,' I said. 'I come off the road back there.' I looked down at the cards. 'Can you tell me if I'll get her back?'

She took my bloodied, swollen hand, pitted with broken glass, in hers.

'What I do,' she explained, waving her free hand across the cards, 'is help you understand your past, *your* damaged past, and assist you along the pathway to a more stable and spiritual future.'

I couldn't quite follow what she was saying. It might have been the drugs and drink, or the concussion I most likely had. I nodded my head in agreement anyway.

'Sounds fine by me.'

She squeezed my hand a little too tightly, considering that it was busted up.

'But in your case, you are not quite ready for such a reading. First you must be cleansed.'

I looked down at the mess and dirt and shit all over me. 'Oh, I can see that. I need to get clean. For sure. I'd like to get this foot seen to, as well.'

She released her hand from mine and rested it on the back of my palm.

'You are a troubled man,' she said. 'Your soul is stuck.'

'Can you help me?' I asked. 'It is stuck, for sure. And I've got this awful ringing in my head that's driving me crazy. Can you get rid of that as well?'

I was now clutching at her hand. I'd frightened her a little. She pulled her hand away from mine, sat back and shook her head.

'No. I'm sorry, but I cannot do that. Not yet.'

I was ready to cry. 'Why not? You just said it's what I need.'

'And it is. But I am not a cleanser. That is the work of others.'

I panicked and grabbed the barrel of the gun and pointed it at her. If she was frightened at all it didn't show. 'What about one of these others? Can't one of them help me?'

She dropped her head. 'No. None of them can help you.' She closed her eyes, raised a finger and pointed towards a small wooden stage, surrounded by heavy curtains, at the far end of the room. 'But he may be able to. If you go to the stairs at the side of the stage, he will see you. Is that what you want? To be cleansed?'

'Yes, please – it's what I want.'

'Well, go quickly. And,' she waited till she had my attention, 'I would leave the gun, if I were you.'

Behind the curtains, the stage was even darker than the hall and I couldn't see a thing. The woman with the cards had sold me a lie, I thought; she'd conned me so she could get rid of me. I was about to walk out when I heard a scraping noise on the wooden floorboards. A shadow moved, and a match was struck. The shadow danced in the low flame, and a candle was lit. And another. And another. The room gradually glowed, soft and yellow. I was standing in front of a man in a long white gown.

He looked to be around my age and had dark hair tied back in a ponytail. He also had a thick beard, and remarkable as it may seem, large breasts. I don't mean man-boobs, but full, beautifully shaped breasts, their cleavage straining to escape the neck of the gown.

He looked down at a wooden stool that somehow appeared between us. 'Please sit,' he said.

I did as he asked, without question, and stared at his breasts as he spoke to me with a voice of honey.

'I will lay my hands on your back. Don't be

concerned when you feel your major organs warming. It is to be expected. If you feel nauseous at any time, or dizzy, that is also normal. If you fear that you may pass out, raise your left arm.' He placed a hand on my head. 'Are there any questions?'

I wanted to ask him about his breasts, but thought better of it. As it was, I couldn't speak. My mouth had gone dry and wouldn't open. He seemed to recognise the problem I was experiencing and offered me a glass of water.

'Drink this. It will help you to relax.'

The water was cold and tasted a little strange, like vinegar. I handed the glass back to him and wiped my mouth.

'Maybe – maybe this isn't for me,' I said, suddenly feeling nervous.

He ignored what I'd said and put his hand back on my head as I shifted in the chair. 'You relax now,' he whispered. He moved behind me and rested both palms against the small of my back.

Straight off I could feel their warmth. A soft ball of heat moved through my body. By the time the dizziness got to me I couldn't have lifted an eyelid, let alone an arm, to help myself. I could feel dribble running down my chin and my forehead being stroked by a gentle hand.

★

I woke cradled in his arms, resting against his breasts. He smiled when I looked up at him. He gently sat me up and massaged the back of my head until I was properly awake.

'You can go now, Luke. It is safe.'

It seemed perfectly natural that he knew my name without me having mentioned it.

The light on the stage slowly faded and the darkness returned. I was alone. It wasn't until I'd walked back through the curtains that I realised that the ringing in my head had stopped and that somehow I was dressed in his white gown.

The church hall was empty and the sun was shining through a window. Outside, the red–dirt road leading away from the church had turned to a sea of mud. I went out through the door and started walking the road, free of pain. Soon I'd passed the lake and the ruins of the mission. A few of the old boys had come back from the dead to greet me. They were singing dirty songs about all the women they'd fucked and called me over for a drink. I waved them off and kept on walking. When I reached the town, I walked straight down the middle of the street. People stopped to gawk, coming out of the stores and standing on street corners watching me. The red dust and mud had settled on the hem of my gown and I looked as if my bottom half had been dipped in blood.

Abraham's old place had been reduced to a heap of smouldering charcoal. I knew what I had to do. I dragged out two blackened bits of wood from the pyre, found some rusting fence wire and bound the pieces of wood together to form a cross. I didn't realise until I'd finished the job that I'd burnt the skin from my hands, although I felt no pain. I picked up the cross and walked to the front of the yard. I found a rock and banged the cross deep into the earth. I looked up to the sky and waited.

THE LOVERS

FRIDAY WAS THEIR DAY. They would turn up just after twelve, before the lunch hour got into full-swing and we ran out of tables. They'd head for *their* table, against the side-lane window and its flowerbox of red geraniums. The couple ordered the same meal, the steaming goulash soup we're famous for. He was tall, tanned and fit-looking and always wore a suit. The waitresses would nudge each other when he walked in and fight over who would take the order. She was built like a sparrow, wore vintage print dresses and had the sweetest face I'd ever seen. They had a habit of eating in silence. It was only after they'd finished and the dishes had been cleared that they'd lean across the table, hold hands and whisper quietly to each other.

When I delivered a tray of food to the table, and returned again to collect the dishes, I'd take my time and listen in on their conversation. They didn't speak a word about insider trading, or a looming legal brief, or whatever else it is that the usual clientele go on about when they're in here throwing back the red and trying to hit on the waitresses.

They appeared to be *the* perfect couple and I never doubted that they were. It didn't stop me fantasising that I might take his place and hold her by the hand and reach across the table myself and kiss her.

When the bell above the café door rang out, announcing their arrival, I would look up at the clock on the wall, lean on the oak bar and whistle to Carmen, the maitre d'.

'They're here. Right on time. And don't they look happy?'

Carmen's a serious hardarse who relies on nothing more than a raised eyebrow to keep the dining room in order. She's bringing up a kid on her own. The boy's father shot through on them before the kid was out of nappies. By Carmen's own calculations she's since been 'fucked over by just about every man in the phone book. My next-door neighbour, who never stops whingeing about the dog shitting on his nature strip; my bus driver who won't change a note, not even a ten, unless he gets a good look at my tits; and the last fella I went out with, who drove my car into a light pole and wrote it off the same day, then sent me a text telling me we weren't suited. So much for e-fucking-disharmony.'

She'd been too burnt to buy my perfect-couple angle, even though it was staring her in the face.

'There's not a couple on this earth that can be that happy,' she'd sneer across the room as they took their seats, 'unless one of them has a bit going on the side. My old man was just like this fella. I'd catch him admiring himself in the bathroom mirror, humming some fucking show tune and preening himself like a rooster. Whenever he behaved that way I could be certain he was on the tear. It was the only time he was happy.'

She'd looked over at the table.

'This one fancies himself just a little too much, so it's most likely him. You wait and see. It'll come out. Always does.'

She smiled wickedly and picked breadcrumbs from my shirt sleeve.

'It wouldn't be all bad news though, would it? You know what I think, Jimmy boy? You fancy her yourself. I bet you think about riding her.' She saw me blush and slapped me lightly on the cheek. 'You always fall for the delicate ones. I wouldn't go at her too hard. You'd hospitalise her.'

I was too busy setting a fresh table to notice that they hadn't turned up at their usual time the following

Friday. Carmen pointed it out to me as I was stacking the fridge behind the bar, with lunch half over.

'What's happened to the love birds today?' she asked, raising *that* eyebrow. 'Something's gone wrong there.'

I looked up at the clock and over at the table. The crockery and glasses hadn't been touched. The table was lonely without them.

'It's only just gone one o'clock. Maybe they're running late?'

'Don't con yourself. They're never late.'

She circled me, stopped behind me and rested her chin on my shoulder. She whispered in my ear and purposely pressed her breasts into my back.

'Don't look so miserable. You know your trouble, Jimmy? You need this *perfect couple*. They give you hope for the future.'

She ruffled a hand through my hair and kissed me on the neck.

'Can I give you some advice?'

'I couldn't stop you if I said no. You're always giving me advice. And none of it's any good.'

She twirled a lock of my hair around her finger.

'Well, let me give you a little more. If you don't want to get hurt in life, in relationships, get your head out of cloud-bullshit-land. You know what your trouble is, Jimmy? Do you really know?'

'No. I've been waiting for you to fill me in.'

'You spend too much time cruising the romance shelves at the video library. All that *Sleepless In Seattle*, *When Harry Met moaning Sally* crap has fucked you up. Your life, Jimmy, lacks perception. You want to know what I watch when I knock off from a long shift here? Worn out, jacked off and stinking of spaghetti sauce and grease?'

I didn't want to know, but Carmen was on one of her rants and there'd be no stopping her.

'I sit down with a cigarette and a drink and watch *Thelma and Louise*. I've got it on an old VHS tape and have just about worn it out. It's one of those "all men are arseholes" flicks. You should watch it. It might teach you something about the real world.'

'I've seen it. It's a leso movie.'

'No it's not. It's definitely an "all men are arseholes" flick.'

I'd had enough. 'Carmen, have you ever considered that you just have an uncanny knack for picking an arsehole out of a haystack? Don't be down on this couple based on your own fuck-ups. I've seen hundreds of couples in here over the years and I'd put my house on these two making it. If I had a house. They're in this for life. Have you thought that maybe they took off early for the long weekend. Don't forget, Monday's a public holiday.'

'Maybe they did. But probably fucking not.'

The next Friday I paced the floor, anxiously waiting for them to arrive. Each time a customer moved towards *their* table I rushed over and waved them away, explaining that it was taken, even though we have a sign above the front door reminding diners that we don't take reservations. I had this crazy idea in my head that as long as the table remained vacant they'd magically appear in the doorway. Though I hadn't heard them discussing wedding plans while eavesdropping on their conversations, every word was whispered with love. I fantasised that they'd gotten married and right now were on their honeymoon, strolling side-by-side along a sun-drenched beach. I didn't mention this to Carmen, knowing she'd spoil my dream by reminding me I was channelling some scene from an ad for an airline.

I never saw the couple together again. After a few weeks I gave up guarding the table under the window, and was only occasionally reminded of them when I served someone at that table. The bell over the front door sounded the arrival of a new customer hundreds of times a day. Mostly I didn't hear it because I was busy running around. But now and then the dull ring of the brass bell would trigger a memory of the lovers. I would look across to the door having imagined them standing arm-in-arm in the doorway. They were never there.

She was the last person I expected to see when I spotted a girl rushing through the crowd outside the café months later. I was parked on an upturned milk crate enjoying a cigarette when she ran by with her head buried in her chest, carrying a sad-looking sandwich wrapped in plastic. I quickly butted out the cigarette and followed her. She stopped at the next corner, waiting for the traffic to clear. I stood beside her and snuck a look at her beautiful face. She looked unwell and had dark rings under her eyes. She'd lost weight too. Her chest rose and fell and she quietly breathed in and out. I wanted to reach out and touch her. I might have been crazy enough to do so if she hadn't stepped off the kerb and threaded her way through the stalled traffic.

She passed by the café most days after that, around the same time she used to arrive with him. Although she never stopped I noticed that she always took a glance at the window. I made a point of standing out the front of the café when she passed. I tried making eye contact but she did not look my way.

Carmen was sitting with me one morning, enjoying the sun, sharing my cigarette and complaining about the boss, when she saw the girl.

'Hey, Jimmy, God, hasn't she changed? The poor girl looks like shit.'

'I think there's something wrong with her. She could be sick.'

144

Carmen took a long, thoughtful drag on the cigarette, passed it to me and blew smoke into the air.

'She's sick all right. She's walking around like a bag of bones and looks like she's forgotten what sleep is. That arsehole.'

'Arsehole? Who?'

'Jesus, you're slow. Wake up. I'd be willing to bet you a week's tips, no wait, I'd put my pay packet on it, that your good old Prince Charming has done the dirty on her. It's like I told you when I first saw them together.'

'You can't know that. She's been away for months. Why would she stay away for so long? Maybe he's the one who got sick and she took time off to look after him. The guy could be dead for all we know. Look at her. She's all in black. Maybe she's in mourning?'

Carmen snatched the cigarette from me, took a last drag and buried the butt in the flowerbox. She was forever screaming at customers for doing the same thing.

'Yeah, she's in mourning, for sure. And it's because he's treated her like a corpse. She's probably been too ashamed to come back to work. Looks like she's had a breakdown to me.'

'A breakdown? No. She's just tired.'

Carmen had her teeth into the boyfriend and there was no stopping her.

'It's more than tired. I've seen that face before. Trust me. He did the dirty on her.' She poked me in the chest. 'Jimmy, I love you. Really. But please,' she poked at me again, 'stop being so naïve.'

Carmen was convinced she was right. Unfortunately she most often was.

I could not believe what I was looking at when the ex-boyfriend turned up at the café a week later. It was a Friday. It was close to noon. And it was raining outside. We were filling for lunch and I was setting a table alongside the open fire when the bell above the door rang. Although I hadn't done so in months I instinctively turned around. He was standing in the doorway shaking the rain from a black umbrella. For just a moment my heart lifted. *They're back*, I thought. They weren't, of course.

He was with another, the *other* woman.

She was tall and thin and dressed elegantly in a cream woollen dress. He glanced across the room at the empty table by the window and strode confidently towards it, lightly guiding his companion with a hand rested on her hip.

I retreated behind the bar. Carmen was running through the Specials board with one of the new waitresses. She'd also spotted the couple. She smiled at me, with all the cruelty she could muster.

'Well, looky-looky who's here. If it isn't deadman-fucking-walking. He looks fit enough to me. Take a look at the suit he's sporting, Jimmy. Didn't buy that off the rack. He's moved up. Promotion would be my guess. And look at her. The price tag on her outfit I wouldn't want to guess. It just has to be a long fucking blonde on the arm for this prick.'

While Carmen's on the short side, I didn't think it was the best time to remind her she's a bottle-blonde.

When none of the staff on the floor moved to serve the couple he stood up and looked with annoyance around the room. Carmen nodded towards the table.

'You going to look after them?'

I studied the deep grain in the wood as I wiped the top of the oak bar, over and over again.

'Not me. I'm busy.'

She snapped her fingers and ordered one of the juniors to the table. I watched the couple from the corner of my eye as he loudly ordered for them both – the goulash soup. I couldn't stomach the insult.

'Did you hear that, Carmen? The soup.'

'Don't worry, Jimmy. I bet you a drink she won't touch it. She can't afford to. You want to keep a wafer figure like that in trim,' she laughed, slapping her own ample arse, 'you dine out on fresh air.'

'He's a fucking arsehole.'

'Finally,' she chuckled, 'you've worked it out. *All* men are arseholes.'

'Not all.'

'Well, most.'

'You're right. Most.'

I was clearing a table on the far side of the room when Carmen rushed over.

'Fuck, Jimmy. I can't believe my eyes. Look, it's the poor girl.'

She was standing in the rain, looking into the café through the side window. Her hair was soaking wet, her black dress clung to her body and her thin arms rested limply at her side. He'd turned his chair away from the window, and the blonde had her head bowed, staring into the red-checked tablecloth. The girl banged loudly at the window with her fists to get their attention. He threw his napkin on the table and called me over. When I didn't move Carmen rested a hand on my back.

'You'd better get over there.'

'He can fuck himself. I'm not going.'

'Please, Jimmy. The girl's upsetting the other customers. Tell him he's a prick, if you like. We don't need his business. Just get over there. I'd go myself, but I'd put a fork in his throat.'

I headed for the table and kept my eyes on the girl outside. She stopped banging and rested a hand on the glass. She looked sadly at him, pleading for some recognition.

'Excuse me,' he demanded. 'Can we please be moved to another table? Away from this window?'

The room was full to the brim.

'I'm sorry. This table is all we have.'

She started banging again, even louder. The blonde flicked a strand of hair from her top lip with a perfectly manicured fingernail. The man half stood, leaned across the table, kissed the blonde deeply on the lips then turned to the girl and smiled. The banging stopped. She wiped tears and raindrops from her cheeks with the sleeve of her dress. She leaned forward, turned her face to the side and rested it against the window. She took a last look at the man who had betrayed her.

When she finally turned and walked away all that was left of the girl was a smudge of mist on the glass.

I walked back to the bar muttering *arsehole* – over and over – from the corner of my mouth.

'Too right,' Carmen nodded.

When the bowls of goulash came out of the kitchen Carmen insisted on taking them over to the table.

'I think I'll throw in a complimentary glass of wine for the two of them.'

'What?' I almost screamed.

She grabbed a pair of tumblers from under the bar and filled them to the brim with the cheapest red we had in stock. She lifted the tray above her head and weaved between the rows of tables like a Flamenco dancer. When she reached the table she practically threw the wine and food down, spilling both across the table.

'Sorry folks,' she sneered. As she walked back to the

bar Carmen gave her death stare to the waiting staff. They knew not to go near the table and clean up the mess.

The couple didn't speak to each other and hardly touched the food on their plates. He got up and walked across to the bar, where Carmen and I were standing behind the register. He pulled his wallet out of his pocket.

'What's the damage?'

Carmen arched an eyebrow.

'The damage?'

'The bill. What's it come to?'

She stared at his open wallet and its array of credit cards.

'No damage. This one is on us. A farewell gift.'

He shook his head and smirked at her.

'Farewell. What do you mean?'

Carmen had picked up a clean wine glass and was polishing it with a linen towel. When he asked her the question a second time she turned to me and nodded towards the table where the blonde was sitting, uncomfortably alone.

'Jimmy, let's get rid of the mess over there.'

The man looked at me, put his wallet in his pocket, collected the blonde and left the restaurant.

They never came back. But the girl did. A few weeks later she walked into the restaurant, around lunchtime early in the week. She looked a lot better than the last time I had seen her. She was wearing a bright red coat and had cut her hair shorter. She looked around the room for a table. I nearly tripped over myself trying to get to her before one of the waitresses.

'Hello,' I smiled. 'Are you alone?'

'Alone?' she frowned.

'For lunch,' I corrected myself. 'Just yourself for lunch?'

'Yes. Just myself.'

There were plenty of empty tables. I looked across to the bar.

'Would you like a table? Or ... how about a seat at the bar?'

She shrugged her shoulders. 'Sure.'

She followed me to the bar where I helped her off with her coat. Underneath she was wearing the same dress she'd had on the day she'd stumbled across her old boyfriend. It looked brighter. She sat up at the bar and rested her chin in her hands, watching as I poured her a glass of white wine.

Carmen suddenly appeared from the cellar where she'd been checking the barrelled beer stock. She looked a little shocked on seeing the girl. We both rested against the back of the bar, watching the girl as she put her lips to the glass. Carmen leaned into me, winked and dug her elbow gently into my ribs.

DISTANCE

I WAITED UNTIL THE TRAIN TRAILED AROUND THE BEND before searching the platform. It was deserted. I picked up my duffel bag, slung it over my shoulder and headed for the nearby street. The station attendant, a sweaty kid around sixteen or maybe seventeen, was resting under the shade of a peppercorn tree alongside an empty car park. He took a drag on a cigarette and then a sip from a soft-drink can as he lazily watched me out of one eye.

I had no idea which way to head, but didn't want to let on that I was lost even before I had started the search. I stopped, put my bag down and looked to the left, at a solitary wheat silo casting a shadow above a derelict homestead, and a few rundown shacks alongside a dirt track wandering into some trees. To the right of me, off in the distance, I could see a service station across the street from a hotel.

A boy wearing a turned-around baseball cap, seated on a slapped-together bicycle made of nothing more than bits of rusted metal, rode into the service station.

A sign of life, I thought, and headed in the same direction.

A swarm of insects – flies, bull ants and some sort of jumping crickets – retreated ahead of me into the long grass on the side of the road. I looked down at the ground. Dust lifted in the air before settling on my recently polished shoes. A truck roared by carrying a herd of scrawny cattle, kicking up more dust. The driver tooted his horn and waved at me through the dirty windscreen. I waved back, then I coughed and spat.

At the service station the boy on the bicycle was using an air hose to remove canes of dry grass from the bike's spokes and chain. It was not a baseball cap the boy was wearing, but a peculiar hairstyle. While a straw fringe of hair lay across his eyes, the sides and back were jet-black.

As I walked by he ran a hand through his hair and smiled, then shot a blast of air in my direction.

Smartarse, I thought, without saying anything.

I had a bone-dry throat and wanted a cold drink. I tried the front door of the shop attached to the service station. It was locked. I put my hand to the side of my face and peered through the glass. I couldn't see anyone. I knocked on the glass. No answer. A notice taped to the inside of the door read OPEN. So I knocked again. Still no answer.

I was about to walk away when I heard footsteps behind me. I turned around and saw a man carrying a large monkey wrench and wearing a pair of overalls covered in dark, congealed grease. He also had smudges of oil over his shaven head.

He raised a filthy hand as if he were about to say something, when he spotted the boy playing with the air hose. He kicked the ground and waved his arms around like he was trying to scare off a mad dog.

'Fuck off, Conway. You never buy nothin' from here. None of you lot. Don't come round here fuckin' with my equipment. Wreckin' it and all. Get goin', you black cunt.'

The boy dropped the hose and jumped on his bike. He obviously had no fear of the man. He slammed a foot down on a pedal and headed straight for the man, who only managed to jump out of the way as the boy was about to crash into him.

'Read your own sign, Huntie-cunt. It says *free air*, you dumb fuck,' he screamed out over his shoulder, then spat on the ground and rode off in the direction of the wheat silo.

'Don't come back here, Conway. Or I'll kick your black arse blue.'

He wiped his hands on his overalls and launched into a short version of his life story.

'Sorry about that, mate. Ted Hunt. I'm the mechanic here. Part owner too. With Bob, the publican. The kid's off the Abo reserve. Fucken trouble, every last one of them.'

'The reserve?'

'Yeah. Government-run place. Used to be, anyway. Supplied the timber cutters for the Forestry Commission. Good workers, my old man used to tell me. Hard to believe now. The Commission's fucked itself now. Bent over and let itself get well and truly fucked up the arse by the Greenies. The reserve's gone too. Officially. Years and years back. They were supposed to have their freedom or something. So you would reckon they'd fucken leave. Well, they haven't budged one inch. You know what we need here? You know?'

He stamped his foot, demanding an answer.

'No. I don't know.'

'An intervention. Like they got up north. We need an inter-fucken-vention. Right here. Fix the cunts up. That would. Get them workin' or get them out.'

He finally stopped talking and looked me up and down.

'You from the government yourself? Agriculture? Water Board? We don't steal no water round here. Only take what comes out of the sky. Which is fuck all.'

He glanced across the road to a dry ditch.

'And from the creek, when it flows. Which it hasn't for years.'

He buried his hands in his pockets, waiting for an answer.

'No, I'm not from the government.'

'Where you from then? You break down on the highway?'

'No. I came on the train.'

'The train,' he cackled. 'Fuck me sideways, mate. Should've let us know you were comin'. We'd have put a brass band on, except that most of the members are dead. Or ...' he looked across the road to the pub, 'or too pissed to blow out a candle. Fuck, no bugger has got off the train here since the breakdown last year. Big group that was too, heading for some flower show in Bendigo. Shit. A flower show? Imagine how much water we waste in this country growin' fucken flowers? I had to feed them all out of the shop here. All I had was Coke, potato chips and stale pies.'

He kicked the toe of his boot into the tarmac.

'So, what are you doin' here?'

'I'm looking for an address,' I explained as I put my hand in my back pocket and pulled out an envelope. It was worn and creased. I handed it to him. 'Do you know where this place is?'

He read the address and screwed his face up.

'What are ya, mate? A goose? This is a Melbourne address. That's where you just come from?'

'Sorry.' I snatched the envelope out of his hand and turned it over. 'I meant this one. On the back.'

He mouthed the address to himself, looked up at me, then back down at the envelope and read it a second time.

'Sure. I know where it is. This is the Munro place.'

'Munro? I'm not looking for Munro. I'm after a Mr Revell. James Revell.'

His face lit up.

'Oh, Jimmy Revell. Yeah, knew him well. A crony of my old man. Drinking mates. Used to manage the Munro grain depot, old Jimmy. Munro had a licence to print money with that grain contract.'

'Used to?'

He looked over my shoulder, towards the silo.

'Yeah. Like I said. Used to. The depot. It went too. With everything else. Wheat train bypasses us for the bigger towns now. You had business with him? Jimmy?'

I looked down at the envelope, stained with his dark fingerprints.

'I'm a relative.'

'Ahh,' he gasped with surprise as he rubbed the end of his chin.

'Relative? I didn't know Jimmy had any relations. He had a girl off the reserve once, years ago. Caused a fucken scandal. And then she fucked off. Left him and the town for dead. They say she was up the spout. One of the few who got away. She went by the name of Winnie. You heard of her? Winnie? Related to her, too?'

I felt a bead of sweat rolling down my cheek and onto my neck.

'A relation?' he prodded.

I took the envelope from him and shoved it into my pocket.

'So where's this place? Munro's?'

'Can't miss it,' he smiled through a mouth of yellowed teeth. 'The silo. Smack bang under the silo, it is.' His expression shifted to gloom. 'But you won't find nothin' there. Nothin'.'

A wire-strung fence surrounded the property, while a metal gate hung from a single hinge. As I opened it, the gate came away from the fence post. I rested it against the post and walked along a pathway, past an old date palm, onto a collapsing front verandah. The windows of the house were smashed in, as was the front door. I began to walk into the house but stopped as I felt a weight press against my chest. I looked into a string of cobwebs hanging from the hall ceiling. Decorative paper peeled from the walls and weeds had grown through gaps in the floorboards.

I sat on the front step of the verandah, took the envelope from my pocket and ran it between my fingers several times before taking out a letter and reading the fading words. The boy who'd had the run-in with the mechanic was back, on his bike, resting against the fence post. I stood up, folded the letter and held it in my hand as I walked towards the gate.

He pointed to the house.

'What are you doin here? This place is private property. The coppers catch you here and they'll whip ya into the gaol. Vandals been round here. Wrecking the place. Coppers are sick of it, they reckon. The sergeant come down the high school last week and says if he catches anyone in the act he'll crack their arse and lock them up.'

'Do I look like a vandal?'

'Na. You look like a priest. Or maybe a probation officer.'

'Well, I'm neither,' I laughed. 'You know much about this place?'

'Who wants to know?'

'Me.'

'Are you a copper, then?'

'No. I'm not a copper. I'm a teacher.'

'Teacher. Copper. Same thing.'

I ignored the jibe.

'You know the man who lived in the house? James Revell?'

He folded his arms across his chest and stuck his hands under his armpits.

'Jimmy never lived in the big house. It belonged to the Munro people. His place is over there.' He nodded in the direction of the collection of shacks. 'The front one was his. Behind that is the kitchen and the wash-house. For the blackfellas, when they worked here.'

I headed across the yard towards the shack. The boy jumped off his bike and followed me. I waited until he had caught up with me.

'Conway. It's Conway, isn't it?'

'Yeah,' he answered, clearly embarrassed. 'After my old man's favourite country and western singer, Conway Twitty. You heard of him?'

'Yeah. Just. You know a lot about this place. How come?'

'I know what my Nan tells me. She used to work here. Cleaning, cooking and stuff. You know Jimmy?'

'No. I don't know him. I'm a relative.'

He looked puzzled.

'You don't know your own relative? I know every relation I've got, from the coast to the hills. Uncles. Aunties. Cousins. All of 'em.'

'You talk a lot, Conway. That fella, back at the servo, he talked a lot. Everyone like that around here?'

'Suppose so. Not much else to do. Nothing wrong with talking.'

I reached the front shack and pushed the door open. There was barely space for the metal-framed bed. I looked down at the stained mattress. The boy tapped me on the shoulder.

'You want to see his grave? He's in the cemetery, just up the road from us. I can take ya.'

'His grave? He's dead?'

'Of course he is. Died out on the road there. A few years back. He had a heart attack comin' back from the pub. I was still in primary school. Nan took me to the funeral. She'd worked with Jimmy for a bit. She was sad for him.'

I leaned against the side of the shack as I felt my legs weaken.

'You okay?' the boy asked.

'Yeah, I'm fine.' I pressed my forehead into a dry and splintered weatherboard, feeling beaten by the trip I had taken, all for nothing. When I looked up the boy was gone.

I walked around the homestead, stopping occasionally to look in through a broken window or pick up a piece of rusted metal from the ground and examine it. When I got back to the front of the house I saw the boy returning down the dirt track on his bike. An elderly white-haired woman with rich brown skin wobbled along beside him. She marched through the gate and walked up to me. Her hands were as calloused as a brickie's and I had never seen a more weathered face.

She gave me a long hard look.

'You been telling Conway here you're a relative of old Jimmy?'

'Yes. I am.'

She dropped her hands onto her ample hips and opened her stance.

'And what sort of relative would you be?'

'What sort? Well, I'm … I'm his …'

She leaned across to me and whispered, 'Your name? What's your name, then?'

'Peter. My name is Peter.'

She nodded her head up and down and quietly repeated my name in a soft voice as she ran her eyes over my face. 'Yes,' she said loudly. 'It's Peter.'

She raised the pale palm of her hand and rested it against my chest. 'Peter. I heard she name you Peter.' She closed her eyes. 'I knew one day you'd be comin'. Thought I'd maybe be dead before you get here. I was sure that one day Peter would come.' She rested her other hand on Conway's head. 'See, Conway. Like I've been tellin' you all.'

She looked along the dirt track she had walked, lifted her arm and pointed.

'We're up here. Me, young Conway here, and the others. You want to come with us? You look worn out, Peter. Come with us. Up home.'

THE MONEY SHOT

VINCENT AND ME ARRANGED TO MEET IN THE CAR park at the 7–Eleven at midnight. 'On the dot,' he'd repeated when he'd called me at the Golden Cue earlier in the night. At half past the hour I was pacing out front of the store doing the best I could to keep warm. There was no sign of him, the 351 tank he drove around town in, or Buster, an associate from way back who he preferred to work with. Buster was top shelf at lifting cars, was a reliable driver, and he could heavy with the best of them. But I couldn't figure why we needed him on this job. We wouldn't be using a hot car, it wasn't a robbery – in the technical sense – and there'd be no aggravation unless we fucked up completely and the Jacks showed.

'Buster could stay home on this one,' I'd put to Vince while planning the job as we walked his dog along the dry creek bed that ran alongside the freeway. It was our office, quiet and out of the way. 'We don't need him.

We end up with a two-way split and a fee for the girl. Makes more sense than a three-way cut. Do the arithmetic, Vince.'

'*Arithmetic*. What does that mean? You watch too much shit on the TV. Fuck the arithmetic, Jackie. And it's math – *do the math*. Buster's never said no to a job. I ask him to do something, he never questions it. Fronts up, does the work and splits. Doesn't splash the dollars around at the Casino. Or on the snatch. And he keeps his mouth shut. Like a steel trap. Can't buy that loyalty. I line up a job, any job, he's in.'

Vince wasn't going to change his mind.

'Okay. He's in. When'd you last see him? He doesn't travel too well on the gear. He could be using.'

'Months back. I've had nothing for him. It's been dry. He's been at me for some work. And he's not using. I wouldn't take him on if he was using. Talked to him on the blower. He's trying to settle down. By the way, the girl we're working with, Juice, she's not in for a fee. She set this up. So she gets a full twenty-five per cent.'

'Fuck. Anyone else? What about the bloke who mows your lawns? How much we paying him?'

'Take it easy, Jackie. This is the laziest quid you'll ever make.'

I couldn't remember money ever being lazy, not the way we had to work for it, at least. It came with stress and aggravation.

I walked into the 7-Eleven, over to the hot food counter, pulled out the last sausage roll from the warmer and hit the *long black* button on the coffee machine. The girl behind the counter was Indian. Or something like it. She had one of those jewelled studs stuck through a nostril. Even in the stained two-sizes-too-big company polo shirt she was wearing, she looked stunning. I tried striking up a conversation about how tiring it must be working the graveyard shift. She smiled as politely as she needed to, handed me my change and went back to watching a Bollywood song and dance on her laptop.

I walked outside and woofed down the sausage roll, took a couple of sips of the syrupy coffee and poured what was left on the ground. It wasn't like Vincent to be late. The job could be off, for all I knew. I never carried a mobile when I worked, in case a mate or some old girlfriend called and I was tracked later on. My legs were turning numb on me. If he didn't pull in by one a.m. I'd hop it home.

I was still hungry and my guts were rumbling. Other than the sausage roll, I hadn't eaten since lunchtime. I rarely ate before a job. Knowing we might have to sit for a while, the last thing I needed on my mind was a gut ache and a badly needed shit. Ducking behind a tree or up a laneway for a piss was no bother, but having to find a bush to squat behind could catch you out – and leave you with a grubby mitt.

I went back into the shop with a hot pie on my mind, realised it could be a poor choice, then walked the aisles and settled on a packet of chocolate Teddy Bears. I was back out front jumping up and down on the spot and munching on a foot when the 351 grunted into the car park. Vincent pulled up in front of me, left the engine running and gave me the thumbs-up. Buster was in the back seat. I walked around to Vincent's side of the car and knocked at the window. He shook his head like he was sorry for keeping me waiting.

'Where you been, Vince? It's the North Pole out here.'

'Sorry.' He nodded towards the back seat. 'We've had complications.'

'Like what? The job still on?'

'It's on. Jump in. We'll talk on the way.'

I hopped in the front passenger seat, turned to Buster and offered my hand.

'Long time no see. How you been, Buster?'

'Good, Jackie. First rate.'

Even in the dull light he did look better than the last time I'd seen him, almost a year back. He was thinner in the face like he'd lost weight, and for the better. He was nursing a blanket in his arms and didn't bother shaking my hand.

'What you got there? You bring your dirty washing, Bust?'

He pulled the blanket away. 'No. It's a kid.'

It was a baby, with big dark eyes and a tuft of hair poking out from under a pink knitted bonnet. I turned to Vincent for an explanation. He shrugged his shoulders and threw his hands up like he didn't want to know. The car was still idling in the car park. Buster and me had worked together on one or two jobs but were not overly familiar. Vince could control him but he had a short fuse and could fight like ten men. I was careful around him and watched my words.

'Is that a baby girl you have there?'

His face lit up like a doting father, which apparently he was, although I'd heard nothing about it.

'Yeah. A little girl. Florence. She's five months old.' He brushed the side of her soft face with a fat thumb. 'What do you think of the name? Florence.'

I'd never given baby names a thought, and didn't care one way or the other. But I wasn't about to insult him and wind him up.

'Yeah. It's a nice name. Like Florence Nightingale?'

'No. Florence and the Machine. Pam, her mum, is a huge fan.'

'She's … Baby Florence … is she yours?'

'Yeah. Mine and Pam's. Our own kid.'

'Ahh, with this job on, little Florence, she's not coming along for the ride, is she?'

Buster apologetically lifted one of his massive fists

and spoke as quietly as an old girl with a bad throat, another surprise.

'I'm sorry about this, Jackie. I really am. But you see, Pam got a call earlier tonight – I was all ready for Vince when Pam's old girl, who lives up in Benalla, took a fall in the kitchen and ended up in Emergency there. Pam's had to take off and look after her. She couldn't take the baby with her 'cause some prick broke into our car a couple of nights back and knocked off the baby seat. And we haven't picked up a new one.'

The baby let out a grizzle and Buster rocked her in his arms.

'I'm on my own with her until Pam gets back. I've cleared this with Vince. Haven't I, mate?'

Vincent didn't say a word. I was keen to prompt him.

'Has he, Vince? Cleared this with you?'

'He has, Jackie. Don't worry. It'll be cool.'

The baby rolled her head from side to side and opened her mouth.

'See that,' Buster pointed, with the knowledge of a midwife, 'with her gob open like that, it means she's hungry. She wants her milk.'

Florence let out a squeal and started to cry. If it had been anyone but Buster nursing the baby I might have made a joke about breastfeeding her.

'Milk? Do you want me to go into the shop and grab a carton?'

'We can't do that, Jackie,' he scolded me, like I was a fucken moron. 'She'd shit through the eye of a needle if you fed her straight milk. Or she wouldn't shit at all. I can't remember which. But it would sure fuck her up. And Pam would cut my balls off.'

He reached behind the front seat and pulled out a pink vinyl backpack covered in yellow daisies. He unzipped the bag, pulled out a full baby bottle and held it to his cheek.

'Good. Still warm. This is proper baby formula, Jackie.' He held up the pack. 'And I bet you haven't seen one of these before? A fucken esky for bubs.'

'No, I haven't had use for one. You, Vince? You seen the baby esky?'

Vincent was picking dirt from under his fingernails, avoiding the obvious problem we had on our hands.

Buster tucked the baby into his armpit and slipped the teat into her mouth. She latched onto it straightaway and sucked like she hadn't been fed in days. He even made baby noises as he fed her. He might have cleared bringing the baby on a joyride with Vincent, but not me. I was taking a risk on the job and was entitled to a say.

'Buster, have you given any thought to pulling out of this one? You know, you and Florence might have been better off taking the night off.'

He shot me a look that cut me in half. Only Buster could do that.

'I need the money, Jackie. For a new baby seat and other stuff. She'll be after a cot soon. And I've promised Pam.' He gave me the eye, to be certain there'd be no argument. 'Anyway, Jackie, I roll with Vince. You know that. I'm Pancho to the Cisco Kid. Isn't that right, Vince?'

'Sure is.' He sounded about as enthusiastic as I was. 'Sure is,' he repeated. 'Hold onto the kid, Bust.'

He put his foot to the floor, reversed the 351, spun the back wheels and tore out of the car park.

Vincent went over the plan as he drove. It wasn't easy concentrating on the detail. I had the radio in one ear, blasting 'hits of the '70s, '80s *and* '90s', and baby Florence screaming out her lungs in the other. She'd demolished the bottle of formula like an alcoholic on the charge and was after more. Vincent struggled to talk over the top of her and a Van Halen guitar solo.

'Juice is in there with him now, at the motel on Park Street. She's going to send us a text on this,' he held up a throwaway, 'with the room number. We crash the door in five minutes after the text comes through. Or thereabouts. We burst in and you start shooting. You got it?'

'No, I don't,' I screamed. I hit the OFF button on the radio. 'I'm sorry, Buster, but I can't hear a thing with the baby in my ear. Can you do something to quiet her?'

He bounced Florence up and down on his knee. 'I'm trying. I've winded her. My guess is that she's still hungry.' He held up the empty bottle. 'There's no formula left.'

'What does she eat?' I asked.

'Mostly this stuff and some cereal and baby biscuits. You wouldn't believe it. She's got no teeth and them biscuits are hard as rocks. She chews on them with her gums. You should see her go. Like Bugs Bunny on a carrot.'

I pulled the packet of chocolate biscuits from my jacket pocket.

'Maybe you could try her on one of these. Can't hurt her.'

'What are they?'

'Chocolate Teddy Bears. My favourite.'

'Hey, fucken mine too.'

He took a biscuit out of the packet, broke off a leg and rested it on the tip of little Florence's tongue. She stopped crying straight off and went at the chocolate.

'She's loving it,' Buster smiled. 'Look at her go.'

'Thank God,' Vincent muttered. 'So, did you get all that, Jackie? You know what to do when we go in?'

'Yeah, I've got it. You kick the door in. I shoot. But can we backtrack a bit. Who's the pick-up?'

'Firstly, we don't have to kick anything in. She'll leave the door unlocked for us. And the pick-up,' he hesitated, 'is some professor from the university.'

'A fucken professor? From the university? The plan was to mark someone with a truckload of money. Some cunt-struck old prick in banking or insurance, you said. Maybe a politician. We never talked about any professor.'

'Take it easy. We tried for the top end of town and got nowhere. Her sister got her a spot working at a club on King Street. She was there for a month and the only bites she got were from low-rung clerks and floor traders too pissed to scratch themselves and too tight to buy her a drink.'

'She should have shown them her tits.'

'She did. Only ended up with more pimply kids chasing her.'

'And she threw it in?'

'She did. And then about six weeks back, she was at the bank and saw this bloke in another line eyeing her like he wanted to fuck her on the spot. She played him right there. Dropped her handbag, he picked it up, she smiled and said, "Ta". They went off for coffee together and she reeled him in.'

Buster broke off another chocolate leg for the baby. He bit the head off the biscuit and chewed on it himself.

'You got more of those, Jackie? She loves them.'

'Yep, plenty, Buster. You look like you fancy them yourself.'

I passed him another biscuit, which he swallowed like a sword.

Vincent pulled into the kerb, opposite a rundown 1960s motel. Its neon sign flashed ARK IEW at us. He pulled a digital camera from his jacket.

'I charged the battery before I left home. It's ready to go. Just point and shoot. All we do now is sit and wait for the call.'

'Are you sure about this, Vince? I don't see us squeezing a fortune out of a fella like this. I've done a few runs through the university, lifting purses from the library, a laptop here and there. Most of them intellectual types walk around with the arse out of their pants and beards storing the leftovers from lunch. Can't tell them from a dero in the gutter.'

'I don't give half a fuck about how they dress. I've done my homework and this bloke's perfect. He's got two kids in private school. That's fifty thousand a year in the till on its own. They live in a double-storey renovated terrace in East Melbourne, a couple of mill, minimum, and they've got a beach house down the coast. Don't worry. He's got plenty. And Jackie, the cream-on-the-cake is his missus. She's old money. The embarrassment would kill her. Her old man is a retired politician. He was a Treasurer or something. So don't worry. This bloke will pay.'

'How'd you get all that info on him, in six weeks?'

'Juice says he's depressed. And likes to talk a lot. Mostly about his troubles.'

'What's the bag?'

'If we go for a one-off, probably twenty. If we can string him out, we might double it. Leave that to me, Jackie. Just be sure you get a good shot of his bare arse along with his happy face.'

'That's if he's fucking her. Maybe he'll back out, seeing he has so much at stake with the wife. He could get cold feet.'

'He's already fucking her. She gave him his first look at it weeks back. Same motel. He rode her like a Cup favourite, she said. Hands and heels. And he couldn't wait to mount up again.'

Buster leaned over the seat and tapped Vincent on the shoulder.

'Have you worked with her before, this Juice chick? She reliable?'

'Yeah. She's a full pedigree. Her granddad was one of the last of the big street bookies. My old man pencilled for him when he was starting out. Our families have been Christmasing together for as long as I can remember. She's like a sister.'

'I wouldn't want my sister on the game,' Buster laughed.

'Neither would I. I said *like* a sister.'

We sat in the car for another half hour without a call

from Juice. Vince checked the phone a couple of times, worried that it might not be working. 'Cheap shit.'

I sensed a complete fuck-up.

'You got a smoke, Vincent? I'm out.'

'Thought you were trying to give up?'

'I am, but it's not working. I got a sore jaw chewing on all that nicotine gum.'

He pulled two cigarettes from a packet and handed me one. He was about to light up when Buster interrupted.

'Fellas, can you smoke outside of the car? You know, with the baby and all, and that passive smoking.'

Vincent looked at him through the rear-view mirror.

'Are you serious, Buster? It's freezing out there.'

'Yeah, I am. I'd be okay with it, just the one fag, but if Pam smells cigarette smoke on the baby's clothes she'll go off her head at me.'

Vincent and me sat on the bonnet of the car and lit up. I pulled the collar of my jacket up around my ears and buried my hands in my pockets.

'He's not the same man, old Buster. What happened to him?'

'Told me while we were driving to collect you that he swore off everything, the drink, pills, the lot, about ten months back. He joined some step program, ten steps, twelve steps, I can't remember how many. And he met this bird, Pam. She's an alkie too. Off it but. They started going out and then moved in together. I have to say he's better for it.'

'He met her ten months back? But the baby's five months old, he said.'

Vincent looked over his shoulder and waved at Buster.

'Don't say a word about it. It's not his kid. The father did a runner as soon as he heard she was up the spout and hasn't been seen since. Buster stepped up.' He dropped his butt on the road and ground it into the bitumen. 'Who would have thought? Buster?'

'Well, not me.'

Back in the car Vincent fiddled with the radio dial, switching from station to station, hoping to calm himself with some quieter music than another marathon guitar solo. Buster's next comment didn't ease the mood.

'Maybe he's a creep?'

'What do you mean? A creep? Who?'

'This fella she picked up. You don't know him from fucken Adam.'

'That don't matter. Juice is a professional. She deals with this stuff every day. If he was a creep she'd smell it straight off.'

'Maybe not. He could be a real sly cunt. You know most serial killers are educated types?'

'He's no killer, Buster. I sat across from her flat last

week. I was watching when he drove up for her. He's skinny as a rake. And looks just like you'd expect from them university types.'

'Like what?' I asked.

'Like he's intelligent and a fucken goose at the same time.'

'Doesn't mean he's not a nutter,' Buster offered. 'Brainy and a goose? That's a bad recipe. I met blokes in jam like that.'

Vince brooded over the discussion. He threw me the camera and grabbed the door handle.

'Let's go, Jackie. Buster, you stay here with the car.'

'And the baby, Vince?'

'Yes, Buster. And the baby.'

We crossed the street to the front of the motel. I could see a bearded fella sitting behind the desk at reception with his back to the door and his head buried in a book. I followed Vincent along the driveway, into an open courtyard surrounded by motel doors, each painted a different bright colour.

'Which one are they in?' I whispered. 'This is like the old days. *Pick-a-Box*.'

He pointed to the rear of the courtyard and a light blue beaten-up Volvo parked in front of one of the rooms. I could see a dull yellow light behind the blind in the window.

'They're in there,' he whispered. 'That's his car.'

'You sure they're in that room?'

'No, I'm not sure, but I seen him pick her up in that car. We'll try the door and run in. You spot them you start taking pictures.'

'Pictures of what? She was supposed to have called you if she was humping him.'

'Maybe she can't call. My bet is something's gone wrong with the phone.'

'So you don't think he's a serial killer,' I laughed, under my breath. 'Buster might be a genius.'

'Shut up, Jackie,' he hissed. 'I don't want you waking everyone up. Just follow me.'

We waited at the door and listened for any action inside the room. All I could hear was Vincent's breathing. He wrapped a paw around the doorknob and tried turning it one way, and then the other. It wouldn't budge. He stepped away and waved at me to follow him, around to a walkway between a high brick wall and the rear of the motel.

'These places have a back door off the bathroom where you put out the rubbish. Our room is three doors along. We'll try the door, or the window if we have to.'

I didn't hold out much hope. Seeing as the front door was locked, I expected the back would be too. I wished I'd stayed home and left the job to Vince and Buster, not that he would have been much help. I figured we'd be going home empty-handed.

As Vince turned the door handle I heard something click. He opened it just a couple of inches and put his ear to the gap. Nothing. He opened it a little more, just enough for us to slip through. He nodded at me to follow. It was dark in the bathroom. I felt my way across the room, praying I wouldn't bump into something and cause a racket. We reached another door. Vince opened it and crept into the room.

A lamp sitting on a bedside table was on. Next to it was an empty magnum of champagne. A huge television set sat at the end of a king-size bed. It was switched on with the sound down, and was showing an old black-and-white movie. Juice lay on top of the bed, naked, wrapped around the body of a man, all white skin, freckles and grey fluffs of hair. They were dead to the world.

'What's she fucken doing?' Vincent whispered in my ear.

'Not humping his arse off, that's for sure,' I answered. 'Looks like the show's over. And the shot.'

'No, it's not. Get the camera out and take a snap of them just like they are.'

He stood on one side of the bed, me on the other. I looked down at the couple. He had lipstick smudges all over his face and more on the side of his neck.

'Not just a head shot, Jackie. Get his hand in the picture, just where it's resting on her arse there.'

'I know what I'm doing, Vince. You're not Quentin Tarantino.'

I stood back and took the shot. The flash hit the professor between the eyes. He reared up, almost knocking Juice off the bed. I could see the attraction. She had a hell of a body. She moaned and squinted into the light. He leaned across her, reaching for the bedside table and a pair of glasses. He fumbled with them, put them on and looked up at me.

'What's going on?' he asked, reasonably calm for a man who'd just discovered a pair of intruders beside his bed. 'Who are you?'

Juice sat up, covering her eyes with one arm as she pulled the sheet over a very expensive boob job.

'Vince, what are you doing here?' she screamed, as if she didn't know what was going on.

He laughed like she'd told him a dirty joke.

'What am I doing here? Fuck off, Juice. The plan. Remember? You and—' he pointed at her companion, 'we're … me and Jackie are supposed to be here. Don't play dumb. What happened to the call?'

I wasn't happy about him using my name. I'd never met Juice, and she had no idea who I was. He could have called me by any name. Like Bob.

She was pissed off with Vince.

'I'm not playing dumb. You're the idiot here. I told you I'd call you *if the job was on*. I'd call you at midnight,

I said, and then again when you got here.' She thumped the mattress. 'Did I call you? Did I fucking well call? No. Because there is no job, Vincent.'

She turned to the professor. He was battling to get a word out.

'I'm sorry about this, Paul. There's been a mistake made. My friend here is not too bright.'

'What is he doing here?' he demanded. 'And what are you doing?' he asked me, pointing at the camera.

'Fuck you, Juice,' Vince screamed. 'Don't think you can fucken scam me. You've gone alone on this. I bet you've found a way to fleece this prick all for yourself.'

'I don't know what you're talking about.' She ran a finger lightly along one of Paul's hairy thighs. 'Ignore this fella, darl. He's an old boyfriend of mine. A bit overprotective, aren't you, Vincie. Means well. You can piss off. And your mate here with the camera.'

Paul jumped out of bed with a sheet wrapped around his chest. He looked a little like a Roman in a toga.

'You must leave now. Both of you.'

Vince picked up the empty champagne bottle. He was about to whack Nero over the head with it when there was a knock at the door.

'See,' Juice hissed. 'You've brought trouble here, with all your noise.'

'I can't be found here … with you,' Paul whined.

She patted his thigh.

'You've already been found, lover boy, by this amateur papa-fucking-razzi.'

The second knock at the door was louder.

'Jackie, get the door,' Vince ordered. 'Don't let them in, even if it's the Jacks.'

I opened the door. Buster was standing on the doormat, nursing baby Florence. His teeth were chattering with the cold.

'Let me in, Jackie. She'll freeze to death out here.'

I followed them into the room. Juice, the professor and Vince stared up at Florence, and her big brown eyes and wisps of dark hair. The bottom half of her face, from the tip of her nose down to her small soft chin, and the front of her pink grow suit, were smeared in chocolate.

'Fuck. What did you do to that kid?' Juice screamed. 'We'll have the welfare in here.'

Buster was more than a little insulted.

'Back off, bitch. There's nothing wrong with her. She's just had a couple of biscuits. Off Jackie here. It's not my fault. This stuff sticks like shit to a blanket.' He turned to Vince. 'Did you get the picture you needed? I've got to get her home. She won't sleep in the car. She's overtired and getting real grizzly.'

Paul crawled across the floor, gathering his clothes.

'I have to leave. I shouldn't have come.'

'Yes, you should have,' Juice purred. 'You did come. Twice.'

There was another knock at the door. The clerk from the front desk burst in without an invitation.

'I just saw someone come in here with a newborn. This is a single room. I want you out.'

He looked down at the floor, at the professor covering his face, up at Juice's marble-sculptured breasts, me with the camera in my hand and Vincent armed with the magnum of champagne. Finally he turned to Buster and the chocolate baby. He put a hand to his mouth.

'What have you done to this baby? This is an outrage. I'm calling the police.'

Buster couldn't have felt more insulted if the man had called him a dog. Nursing Florence in one arm, he wrapped his free claw around the clerk's neck and lifted him off the ground.

'You're calling nobody, shit for brains. I've done nothing with this kid but take good care of her. You got that?'

The clerk couldn't answer while he was being choked to death. I didn't want Buster killing him, and us getting done for murder.

'Ease up on him, Bust. Throw him in the bathroom and lock the door. We have to sort something here. I'll clean the kid up for you.'

'Let me take care of her for you,' Juice offered, 'I love babies.'

Buster squeezed a little harder on the clerk's neck. He didn't look too comfortable about giving up the baby. Vince walked across the room and tapped him on the shoulder.

'Come on, Buster. She might not look it, but Juice is real maternal. And I don't need this bloke listening in on our business. Put him in the bathroom. Please, mate.'

Buster released the clerk. He fell to the ground spluttering. Vince took the baby and handed her to Juice while Buster dragged the clerk into the bathroom and kicked the door shut.

Vince waved the magnum around like a baseball bat.

'Okay, professor. Down to business. We've got a nice shot of you cuddling up to your girlfriend. You can have it splashed all over the place, with copies sent to your missus and the news. Or,' he slowly twirled the magnum in the air as if it was a magic wand, 'you can pay us for the picture. You can keep it in your wallet or ditch it. Your choice.'

I could hear a siren off in the distance, getting closer. The baby was trying to latch onto Juice's nipple as she wiped Florence's face and hands with a tissue. The professor was defiant.

'This is blackmail. I will pay you nothing.'

Vince stood over him and lifted the bottle in the air.

'Call it what you like. But you'll pay, cunt. Name a price or I'll smash this over your head.'

The professor covered his face with his hands – as a blue swirling light lit the room.

'The Jacks!' Vince screamed. He dropped the bottle and headed for the back door. 'Jackie. Buster. Go. Go.'

I followed Vince, Buster grabbed the baby from Juice and ran after us. We raced along the walkway, down the side of the motel and across the road. I dropped the camera and turned to pick it up. A speeding tow-truck was heading for Buster and Florence. Swerving to miss them, the driver ran straight over the camera, smashing it to pieces. I watched his tail-lights vanish into the distance. Vince looked down at the broken bits of plastic and metal scattered across the road.

'Fuck,' he whispered. 'There goes the money shot.'

'I don't reckon he would've paid up anyway,' I tried consoling him. 'Stubborn prick.'

'Anyway,' Buster offered, 'they might be in love.'

'Love?' Vince spat. 'They couldn't be in love. She's a prostitute, Buster. Been under everything but the *Titanic*.'

'Don't matter,' Buster shot back, smooching Florence on the cheek. 'If there's hope for me, there's hope for all of us. Juice in there. The professor. And you. Yep. There's even hope for you, Vince.'

SNARE

Nothing much moves around here but the trains. We're two stops off the end of the suburban line. The trains come and go every half hour, in both directions. A little longer on Sundays. Forty minutes, sometimes an hour if they're running late. I time them on my watch and write everything down in the notebook I carry around. Then there are the country line and goods trains. They can thunder by the back fence at any hour, rattling the dishes and knives and forks and spoons in the kitchen cupboards. A couple of times we've had pictures knocked off the walls.

We've been here for six years, from when I was eight. My mother ran away from my dad. I don't know exactly why. She's never told me and doesn't want me asking. I remember that the police were often at our house. And he kicked the front door in one time, when she tried locking him out.

That's all I can tell you. Except that she blames him for my stutter and my eyes blinking. Said so to the doctors at the hospital I went to for years. I'm supposed to be on medication. I was for a long time. When I started high school she said I was responsible enough to look after the pills myself, so I stopped taking them. I flush them down the toilet or feed them to next-door's cat. It doesn't seem to mind. I still blink too much now and then and get stuck on words, but not when I write them down. I don't speak much unless I have to.

The first night here we slept on the kitchen floor because the other rooms were full of rubbish and a sort of scratching sound that had to be rats and mice. A diesel going by the back fence shook the house so bad I thought it was an earthquake until I heard the whistle of the train heading for the crossing on the highway.

With some help Mum fixed up the house. We dragged the rubbish out of the rooms, made a bonfire in the yard and burned the lot. Grandpa drove down from his farm and stayed with us for a few weeks, the old van loaded with tools and paint and pieces of wood. He worked hard, fixing windows and doors, and plastering and painting the inside. At the end of his stay I sat on my bed in the freshly painted front room and listened through the open window to them talking, out on the front verandah, holding a glass of beer each. After all the work he'd done he tried talking her into selling the place and moving to the farm with him. When she said no, for the third time, he went into his overalls pocket and handed her some cash.

'Get the floors sanded with that. I'd do it myself, but my back wouldn't last. We can work on the outside paint job later in the year when it's warm.'

The next week I helped her empty the house of furniture and a man came around in a van with *Sam the Sandman* painted on the side. He took the years of scratches and stains out of the wooden floors with a fearsome machine and varnished them like new. Sam had the quietest voice I'd ever heard and soft curly hair and a beard to match. He came back a couple of weeks later to check that she was happy with the job and then turned up a couple of days after that and started scraping the dry and blistered paint off the weather-boards. When I got home from school that night he was still working, and stayed on for dinner. Before too long he was sleeping over.

Except for the trains it's dead quiet in our street. Our neighbours are mostly old Greeks and Italians. Theo, our next-door neighbour – not the one with the cat, he's on the other side – has lived by himself since his kids left home and his wife died. He gives us vegetables out of his garden. I've been working for him for the last two years. He offered me the job by showing his knotted, bony wrists over the front fence.

'I have the arthritis. Work my arse off for the factory. My hands are fucked up, all. You clean the chooks couple days a week, shovel shit, hose, water. I give your mother eggs, fresh. Every day. You dig in the garden I give vegetables. Tomato. Beans. Everything.'

So I clean out the chook shed on Sunday and Wednesday mornings before school. I worked out quick that Theo is lonely. He sits on an overturned bucket, watches me work and smokes as he talks.

'You know, when we were at factory, Aussie boys bludgers. All of them. All the time. Drink, drink, drink. Do fucken nothing. You work hard. You good boy.'

I sometimes try answering him but my tongue won't work and I spit bits of words out like chips of wood. Theo doesn't mind.

'You get stuck. No worries. I speak. You listen.'

He sends me home with a cloth bag full of eggs. I wash my face and hands then run down to the highway for the bus and ride the half hour to school. I keep to myself, up the front behind the driver. The Islander boys run both the bus and the schoolyard. They take no shit. There are also the Vietnamese boys, and the Africans, but not enough of them to take on the Islanders, even if they joined forces. I have no friends at school and hang out with the losers nobody wants. We don't move far from the patch of grass near the front office, where we can be seen and it's safe.

Six months back Theo offered me a new deal. There's a grain store further along the railway line. It's covered in years and years of pigeon shit and looks like a giant candle slowly melting into the ground. Theo told me that when he was first married and moved out here with his wife he would head down there after work and catch pigeons in a snare he'd made.

'I break the neck and pluck. My missus, Gloria, she cook straight off. Nice. You like the chicken meat? This is better.'

Theo said he would give me a dollar a bird. He taught me how to catch them, practising in his back-yard. He turned a cardboard box upside down and lifted it on one side using a long stick with a line of string tied to it. He put a small pile of rice under the box and made a trail of rice leading away from the box.

'The bird, she comes,' he explained, with the end of the line of string twirled around his finger. 'She takes food from the ground.' He bobbed his head forward like a bird would peck at the grains of rice. 'And then she goes under for the food. You wait. Wait. Pull.'

The stick came away from the box and it closed over the pile of rice.

I found catching pigeons easy and would return to his back gate with a pillowcase full of wildly flapping birds, which didn't please him.

'You catch. You kill. Quick.'

He showed me how to wring a bird's neck, which I was supposed to do as soon as I had trapped it.

'Is better for the bird.'

I found that my blinking stopped when I concentrated on a bird moving towards the box, following the line of rice. One day I spilled more rice than I should have and the bird, a grey, speckled with silver, green and purple, headed for me instead of the box. It was at my feet pecking at the spill when I snatched it from the ground. After that I didn't use the snare at all but caught the birds in my hands.

I was soon spending most weekends in Theo's back garden, or at the granary stalking pigeons. When he told me he was going away for a week, to visit one of his daughters for Greek Easter, I didn't know what to do with myself. I had the chooks to look after but no one to talk to and there was no point in catching pigeons, on account of Theo's strict rule – 'You catch the bird, you eat the bird, same day.' If I went out catching birds while he was away they would be on the nose before he got back.

I got the wanders that weekend, roaming wider than usual. I walked the train line in both directions, trailing through empty factories and bombing stones into the oily channel running next to the line. I ended up behind the abandoned bowling alley across from the railway station car park. It had been locked and bolted for years. The windows had been nailed over with sheets of iron and the outside walls were covered in graffiti, mostly tags left by the Islander gang, XXX–RATED was the tag they went by.

I walked around the outside of the building and stopped at a window that had a corner of iron sheeting lifted. There was enough room for me to wedge my fingers between the sheet of iron and the window frame. I pulled on the iron. The rusty nails popped and the iron came away in my hands and fell to the ground. I stuck my head through the window. The air smelled of rotten meat and dirty water.

I looked around to be sure nobody had seen me and climbed through the window, landing on some broken glass. The skylights in the roof made it easy to see where I was going. At the end of the bowling lanes the pins, covered in dust and cobwebs, stood to attention. Bowling balls sat in the racks, ready to go, and a huge disco ball hung from the ceiling above the centre lane. Only the shoe rack was empty. Someone must have taken a fancy to them.

I tried one of the bowling balls for size. It was too heavy. I put it back in the rack and picked up another, a red ball. I'd never bowled before and wasn't sure what to do. I stuck the ball under my chin like I'd seen a bowler do on television one time and concentrated on the pins, in the same way I had done when snatching pigeons. My blinking stopped. I slipped on my run–up and dropped the ball. It crashed to the boards, bounced into the gutter, rolled down the lane and wobbled by the pins. I picked out another ball and stuck it under my chin again. This time I didn't let go until I reached the bowling line, marked by a row of brass diamonds in the floor.

I slung the ball as hard as I could and listened as it rumbled and echoed, over and over and over, before crashing into the pins. Most of them went down straightaway. One of the back pins wobbled from side to side then fell, hitting another and leaving only two pins standing. I was so happy I whooped out loud.

I played every lane until the last pin had dropped and my bowling arm was worn out. I was thirsty and hungry and headed for the vending machines in the foyer. The potato chips, lollies and chocolate machine were covered in rat shit. Empty packets lay in the bottom, chewed to confetti. The soft-drink machine looked a better bet but I couldn't get to the cans without smashing the front of the machine. I picked up a bowling ball, spun around in a circle like a discus thrower and hurled it at the machine. The glass front shattered into bits.

I emptied the machine of drinks, careful not to cut my arm on the jagged glass, and sat the cans on the floor. I counted them up. I had twenty-two cans. I picked up a can of lemonade and wiped the dirt from the top on my T-shirt. I opened it and took a sniff. It smelt okay and there were bubbles. I put my lips to the can and tipped it back, just a little. It was sweet and sticky and warm. I finished the can off and fiddled with the money slot on the side of the machine. I could hear coins rattling around inside but had no idea how to get it open. I whacked the machine with the bowling ball a couple of times. Nothing happened. I bowled the ball across the foyer. It ran down the stairs into one of the lanes and stopped in the gutter.

I knew I wouldn't be able to carry all the cans of drink home, so I lined ten up in a bowling-pin formation and was about to bowl them over when a pin whizzed by my head, bounced off the wall and ricocheted into the side of the lolly machine. I turned to see where it had come from. It was the Islander boys, six or seven of them, standing in the shadows of lane ten. The biggest boy, Israel, was a year in front of me at school and was feared by everyone, even the boys in years above him. He had an older brother in gaol. Everybody knew that one day he would follow him. He had a wild Mohawk hairdo that he'd done himself and an ugly scar below one eye; some said from a knife fight.

The other boys formed a V-shape behind him as he walked towards me. He pushed me in the chest with

one of his paws and bent forward, staring me in the eye.
My blinking went off the radar. The more I tried to
stop it the worse it got, like window wipers at double
speed.

'What you doing here, in our place? You skinny
freckle-faced motherfucka skip. And stop your winking
at me like some fucked-up spastic.'

When I didn't answer he pushed me again.

'Fuck you, nut boy. This belongs to us. xxx crew.
Say something before I show you some kick.'

'He can't talk, Issie. He's retarded.'

It was Moses. Israel's younger brother. He was in my
year. Israel spat at my feet.

'Can't fucken read either. Our brand is swarming
this place. You fuck off home, runt.'

He pushed me again. I slipped and fell onto my arse.
I cut my elbow on a broken piece of glass. I only cried
when I saw the blood pouring out. The boys laughed
at me until Moses spotted the blood.

'Hey, come on, man. He's hurt.'

Israel looked a little worried himself. 'Get up, retard.
You being a bitch.'

The blood ran down my arm onto the floor.

'Look at the cut.' Moses pointed to it. 'We're fucked
if he reports us.'

Israel whacked him across the face. 'Shut it. Giving
him ideas.'

He lifted me off the ground and put his arm around me, like he was my best friend. 'You say anything about this and I'll skin you. Got it?'

All I could do was nod my head.

'Now fuck off home like a cry-baby and come up with a good story.'

I told my mum I fell on the railway tracks. She banned me from going further than Theo's place for a month, which wouldn't stop me getting around as she was always working and had no idea where I got to during the day. As she washed and bandaged the wound she asked me if there was something wrong.

'I'm worried about you, Tom. You spend more time over at Theo's than you do here. I don't mind. He's a nice old man, but ... are you unhappy? With Sam being here?'

I shook my head, 'No.'

'Would you like to talk to him? Maybe there's something you'd rather talk over with him? You know, man to man?'

I shook my head again. Sam was okay, but I didn't want to talk to him about anything.

Mum let me miss the final two days of term. I had a little over two weeks before I would have to face Israel again. When Theo came home from Greek Easter and

I told him I'd fallen on the railway tracks he knew I was lying.

'Bullshit story. You sit. You speak. Slow. You tell Theo. I will fix.'

I sprayed and stuttered but got the story out in the end. I started crying when I told him I was afraid to go back to school and face the gang. He patted me on the shoulder and clicked his tongue against the roof of his mouth, the same way that he spoke to the hens.

'You must go to school.'

I shook my head, furiously, from side to side.

He put a hand under my chin and made me look at him. 'I make you present for them boys. You feed chooks and I go in shed. We work together.'

I sat in the pen with the chooks until Theo called me.

'Come.' He was holding a length of pipe in his hand. He handed me a lead marble. 'Take.'

He pulled a large firecracker and a cigarette lighter from his pocket. He handed me the firecracker. The layers of paper were flaking away and the firecracker was falling apart. I wouldn't have been surprised if it went off in my hand as soon as I lit it. He clicked his fingers.

'Give me marble.' He dropped the marble into the pipe. He pointed at the cracker. 'You light. Push in hole. Here.'

He showed me the open end of the pipe. I lit the cracker and shoved it into the end of the pipe.

He rested the pipe gun on his shoulder like a miniature rocket launcher and aimed it in the general direction of his tin shed. I heard a loud bang and a ringing sound. Smoke poured from both ends of the pipe. Theo dropped the pipe to the ground and walked over to the shed. He stuck a finger in the neat round hole in the tin.

'See? Good job.'

He went back into the shed and came out with a leather bag with more lead marbles and firecrackers inside. 'You practise, practise. Then boys come and give trouble, you shoot. Send them away.' He shrugged his shoulders. 'You no kill any. But you hurt, you frighten, and you free then.'

Theo had gone crazy. Maybe I couldn't kill Israel with the pipe gun but I could take his eye out. And I would be in big trouble. He could see that I was worried.

'You have choice. Number one, you do nothing. They bully. Any time they see you. Bully. Bully. Again. Fuck again.' He put his hands on my shoulders and shook me, just a little. 'Number two,' he rested one hand on my heart, 'you say, "Fucken no more," and you fight. Okay?'

'Okay.'

I took the bag home and hid it under my bed. I didn't want to hurt anyone with it but I was excited about trying out the marble gun. The next morning I tucked the bag in the front of my jacket and left home by the back gate as soon as my mother had gone to work. I walked the line to the granary.

I practised loading the pipe with the marble and sticking the cracker in the hole, without lighting it, until I could do it all quickly. I balanced a battered old paint tin on a fence post, took a deep breath, lit the cracker on the ground, shoved the marble in, followed by the cracker and aimed the gun at the tin. The blast popped my right ear. I didn't know I'd hit the tin until it started weeping red paint from a hole near the bottom.

I fired off a couple more shots. I had plenty of marbles left but only two firecrackers. I put everything back in the bag then crossed the tracks and headed home. As I rounded a bend across from our fence, I spotted a boy and girl up ahead on the tracks. He was much bigger than the girl and looked older. He dragged her by the arm. She screamed at him to leave her alone.

'Stop it, will you? Please.'

She fell on the ground and wouldn't move. He wrapped her in a bear hug, pinning her arms to her side.

'I'll stop when we're finished.'

He lifted her off the ground and struggled with her,

dragging her into a line of trees and scrub. I fell to my knees and crept along behind them. When he reached the trees he threw the girl onto the ground and stood over her.

'You move, you say a word, make a sound, and I'll kill you.'

I hadn't seen either of them before. He had a shaved head and tattoos on his neck. She was Islander.

He undid his fly, put his hand in his pants and rubbed at his cock. I crept a little closer, as quietly as I could. I tucked the length of pipe under my arm and put a lead marble in my mouth. I stood up and held a firecracker in one hand and the cigarette lighter in the other. The girl saw me and looked up from the ground. He turned around. He was giving his cock a good tug.

'Hey. Fuck off. Before you cop a kicking.'

When I didn't say anything he laughed.

'Please yourself, cunt. Watch and learn. What the fuck's that?' He screwed his face at me, seeing me light the cracker.

'You come near me with that and I'll cave your arse in. And then hers.'

I stood perfectly still for a second and remembered what Theo had said to me. I rammed the lit cracker in the back of the pipe, took the marble out of my mouth, dropped it in the front of the pipe and aimed at his head. I shut my eyes and turned my head away from the blast. He cried out like a dog booted in the guts with a steel-cap. When I looked he was rolling around on the ground, screaming out and holding his hands to his face.

'Jesus. Fuck. You shot me.'

I hurled the pipe gun at him. The girl jumped up and stopped next to him. She stomped on his back with the heel of her shoe.

'Dirty bastard.' She kicked him again and ran after me.

I led her to the laneway behind my street. We ran until we reached the back gate. 'In here.'

I kicked the gate open and bolted it behind me. We were both puffing like mad. She had a deep scratch on her neck and blood on her white skirt. She had chocolate-coloured skin and an Afro hairdo.

'Who are you?' she barked, like I'd been the one who'd attacked her.

I tried getting my name out – Tom – but couldn't. When we'd both got our breath back she told me her name was Angeline and thanked me for saving her. She said she'd seen the older boy at the station when she got off the train and didn't know he was following her until she heard him behind her when she was taking a short cut across the tracks.

'What a fucking creep. Wow. You shot him. He fucking deserved it. Where do you go to school, anyway?'

'Hu … Hu … High.'

'I bet you know my older cousin then. Israel. Everyone knows Issie.'

The first day back at school for the new term I stayed away from Israel and his boys, until lunchtime, when I noticed them walking towards me, across the school ground to the losers' patch of dirt. Israel sat down next to me, cocked his baseball cap back on his head and put his arm over my shoulder, just like he had the day at the bowling alley. I waited for him to snap my neck.

'I never thought you'd have the balls to be a shooter, retard. You saved my cuz, Angel, from that motherfucka pedo. You a soldier, man.'

He slapped me on the back. 'You done well. Moses and me, and the boys, we giving you the green light for that one. You know what that is? The green light?'

I shook my head.

'You don't worry about that, Bro. You don't say nothing much. But you a shooter. Fucken ice cool shooter. The green light is simple. It's like what the big boys do. All them hoods on the TV. It means you get no more trouble from any motherfucka at this school.'

He hugged even tighter.

'Your shit is Issie's shit.'

He stood up and waddled away, his troops in single-file behind him.

When I got home from school that night old Theo was hanging over his front gate, waiting for me. He looked worried.

'How you go, little bird? You have trouble from bully?'

'No,' I smiled.

'Good.' He clicked his tongue. 'Bang. Is best.'

KEEPING GOOD COMPANY

A GOOD NIGHT'S SLEEP WAS HARD TO COME BY. I'd get into bed around nine-thirty or ten o'clock and read for a few minutes before nodding off. The problem was that I'd wake a few hours later, around one in the morning. I'd toss and turn for half an hour or so before giving up on sleep and would turn the reading lamp or the radio on to ease my anxiety. That activity would take me through to around four in the morning, when I would abandon the bed altogether and head to the kitchen, make myself a cup of tea and collapse on the battered couch alongside my ageing Staffordshire terrier, Ella, and the stray one-eyed black and white cat I'd recently inherited. I'd rest an arm on the snoring dog, nurse my mug of tea on my lap and wait for the sun to come up.

On the morning of the accident I'd managed to sleep in, if you could call it that. I'd got through most of the night and was woken by a noise in the bedroom around five in the morning. I flipped onto my stomach and buried my face in the pillow. A little while later I heard the noise again; tap-tap, tap-tap. It was similar to a sound from a few weeks earlier, when I'd heard a knock at the bedroom window in the middle of the night. I'd hopped out of bed and drawn the curtains to one side, to see a scrawny cat sitting on the window ledge. When I growled at it to piss off it meowed and stuck a paw against the glass. I then knocked on my side of the glass with a knuckle to shoo it away. Eventually the cat jumped from the ledge and vanished behind a bush in the front garden.

I'd been back in bed for five minutes when the tap-tapping started up again. The cat was back. By the time I'd grabbed my dressing gown and opened the front door it was sitting on the mat. When I tried nudging it off the mat with my slippered toe it defiantly stared up at me, hissed loudly, then skipped by me. I ran after it, down the hallway and into the kitchen where it had already sniffed out Ella's bowl and was getting stuck into what was left of her dinner. Ella spied the cat out of one eye but couldn't be bothered moving from the couch. A few years earlier, when she was young and fit and angry, she would have jumped down from the couch with a vicious bark and driven the cat from the house. These days she was too slow and comfortable to bother. From that night on, Ella and the cat, which I refused to name, hoping to discourage it from feeling at home, negotiated each other from a safe distance before eventually settling for the shared warmth of the couch.

I heard the sound again, lifted my head from the pillow and stared up at the ceiling. We'd had rats in the roof the year before, although the noise they'd made was a scratching. We'd always had rats in the house and around the garden, sometimes a solitary rogue, and at other times an invasive colony. And they'd been impossible to get rid of. The task was made more difficult because my wife, Lois, was a vegetarian and an animal lover. Tired of listening to the rats scamper around inside the roof of a night, enjoying some sort of rat orgy, I suspected, I came home from the hardware store one afternoon with a set of traps, various poisons and other contraptions that promised extermination. Lois was horrified and screamed that she would have me harassed by the animal liberationists who had moved in up the road if I put as much as a sprinkling of cheese on a single trap. Without protest I threw the traps in the garbage, along with most of the poisons. But not all of them.

I waited until she was out one night at a dinner party with colleagues from work. I went into the garage, carried the stepladder back to the house, lifted the manhole from the ceiling in the bathroom and hurled a dozen small sacks of rat bait throughout the darkened roof space. Over the following weeks the sound was reduced to an ever-slowing patter of rat feet that sounded like they were wearing knitted socks. Lois woke me early one morning, claiming she'd heard a whimper coming from somewhere in the roof. We sat up in bed, shoulder-to-shoulder, actually touching, and listened closely. I could hear nothing.

'You must have had a bad dream,' I told her, feigning some care, before turning onto my side and contemplating the suffering I'd caused.

I listened more closely when I heard the tapping for the third time. It was not coming from outside the front window or in the roof. It was a knock at the front door. I staggered from the bed into the hallway, turned on the porch light and opened the door, shocked to see my elderly next-door neighbour, Jim Egan. He looked in a terrible state, shivering to death and wearing a motley outfit – a woman's floral dressing gown and a muddied pair of work boots. He had a Carlton football beanie perched on his head and a look of fear in his eyes.

Jim leaned forward and studied my face.

'Matthew? Is that you, Mattie boy?'

I rubbed the sleep from my eyes.

'Yeah. It's me, Jim. What are you doing here in the middle of the night? It's freezing outside.'

He looked up at the moon disappearing behind heavy clouds.

'It's not night. It's near morning.'

I'd lived next door to Jim and his wife, Nora, for more than twenty years. He'd been a remarkably fit and alert ninety-year-old until two years ago when his memory began to fade. Nora died six months later after an innocuous slip in the back garden. Jim's own health, both mental and physical, had deteriorated faster since then. He would have been in a geriatric home by now, if it were not for his doctor, a local GP almost as ancient as Jim himself. He was happy to write whatever prescription Jim needed in order to continue battling along on his own.

A blast of wind lifted Jim's dressing gown, exposing his bony pale knees. I took him by the arm and helped him into the hallway. He rubbed the palm of his hand against his chest.

'I've got this pain here, and I can't find my heart medicine any place. We need to get going to the all-night chemist and get myself fixed up with some tablets.'

He placed one hand on the wall for support and looked like he was about to keel over. I didn't want him dying on me.

'Jim, maybe you need to go to hospital? I can drive you. I've still got the VW. Or perhaps we should call an ambulance?'

He shook his head with as much strength as he could summon.

'We don't need no hospital. The doctors there are all foreigners. They don't know how to look after me. I just need my tablets.'

On several occasions over recent months Jim had called me on the telephone and asked for my help. He would complain that his back had gone and he could not get out of bed and go to the toilet or dress himself. I would have to help him out of bed and walk him around the kitchen until he 'got up a bit of steam in the boiler', as Jim liked to put it. Once he got his bones moving he would have me make him a cup of tea and a slice of toast, and sit and talk with him at the kitchen table. He usually knew who I was, although he'd mistaken me both for a nephew of his who'd been dead for years, and for the plumber who'd recently unblocked his kitchen sink.

I guided Jim along my hallway and sat him on the couch between the animals and began making him a cup of tea. Either he or Ella let out a long deep fart. They looked accusingly at each other. I noticed that Jim had stopped rubbing his chest and wondered if he'd been faking it. He had a habit of feigning injury or illness for company. I put two sugars in his milky tea and handed him the mug.

'How's the pain in the chest, Jim?'

'Oh, a bit better. Maybe,' he added a little slyly. 'Could come back any tick, though.'

He sipped at the tea and looked around the room.

'Where's the wife? Got her hidden away?' He laughed.

'She's gone, Jim,' I answered, without embarrassing him by adding that I'd provided him with the same information many times before.

'That's no good. My missus, she died too.' He scratched his head, mining for information. 'Some time back. What took your wife?'

'Her boss from work, Jim. She didn't die. She left me for another man. Six months ago.'

'Left you?' He was outraged. 'The bloody bitch.'

He shook his head in disbelief and patted the cat.

'What's her name again?'

'The wife? Lois.'

'No. Not her. The cat?'

'Doesn't have one. You can name it if you like. I don't know if it's a boy or a girl. I haven't looked.'

'Oh, she's a girl, this one,' he smiled as he patted her gently on the side of her neck. 'I can tell by her mood. The quiet type. Like my Nora.'

I sat opposite him in one of the kitchen chairs and

watched as he studied the cat's face and finished his tea. He drained the bottom of the mug, looked across at me, and smiled.

'Lois, you say? Don't know that it suits a cat.'

He suddenly got to his feet, frightening the cat. It jumped from the couch.

'What are you doing, Jim? You don't have to go. It's wet out there.'

He walked across the kitchen, with a straighter back than I'd seen on him in months. He stopped at the sink and looked out the window into the darkened garden. He coughed and cleared his throat.

'Ever get lonely, Matthew?' he asked, with his back to me.

I stood up from my own chair, put my empty mug on the bench and raised both arms above my head, unsure of why I'd done it, except that Jim's question made me feel anxious.

'Yeah, I do, Jim. Sometimes. Me and Lo— my wife and I were together for more than twenty years.'

'Nora and me,' he turned around and rubbed an eye with a finger, 'we both know I forget stuff now and then, but not the stuff that matters. We were married for sixty years. That's a long time.'

I buried my hands in my dressing-gown pockets.

'It sure is, Jim. A long time.'

He smiled and reached for my arm.

'You know I haven't got long?'

'Long for what?'

'Don't go doggo on me, Matthew. You're smarter than that. I've been on this Earth twice as long as you have. And I'm about three times as crafty. I'm dying, boy.'

'You don't know that, Jim,' I answered, for no good reason.

'I know it, all right. That's why I'm going near no hospital. One look at me in there and they'll have the priest and undertaker on standby.'

He rested his hands on my shoulders.

'Look at me.'

Although his eyes were clouded in an opaque film, a spark of blue remained.

'I've got a list of stuff I want to do before I go.' He squeezed my shoulder with his right hand. 'Before I drop down dead. Will you help me with my list?'

'If I can, Jim,' I answered, with little enthusiasm. 'Have you written it down, the list?'

'Not yet. But now that you're in agreement I'm going to get onto it. We best make a start. I could go anytime. Anytime. What will we do first?'

'I don't know, Jim. It's your list.'

Ella rolled onto her back. The cat jumped onto the couch and sniffed at her belly. Jim walked back to the couch, sat down and patted the cat. The three of them looked made for each other. I thought he'd lost track of our conversation until he raised a finger in the air.

'Ice-cream.'

'Ice-cream?'

'Yep. Chocolate ice-cream. I haven't had it in years. My diabetes. Nora wouldn't let me touch it. Number one on my list.'

He slapped his hands together, startling Ella, who sat up and looked at me for reassurance.

'That's what I want, some chocolate ice-cream.'

It was a simple request. I felt relieved that I wouldn't have to escort him on some pilgrimage or take him skydiving, or something worse, like a visit to a massage parlour.

'That's good, Jim. I'll nick down the supermarket later this morning and drop a tub into you.'

'Later this morning? That's no good. We have to go now.'

'Now? What's the rush?'

'Now. I don't want to be a bother, Matthew, but geez, I'd love some of that ice-cream right this minute. I can taste it in my mouth. And,' he shrugged his shoulders and rubbed his chest again, 'who knows? I could drop off just like *that*.'

He tried clicking his fingers together but couldn't quite manage it.

I didn't want to leave him alone, and there were good reasons for not taking off for the supermarket on a cold and dark morning just for ice-cream, but I couldn't bring myself to refuse him.

'You'd have to come with me, Jim, in the car.'

He slapped a hand against his thigh.

'I'm ready to go when you are.'

I looked at his lurid dressing gown and down at my dull and worn brown corduroy number.

'Maybe one of us should get dressed.'

He was already on his feet.

'No need for that. We should get going. You never know, they might run out!' He smiled, suddenly full of energy.

Ella's ears pricked up as soon as I grabbed the car keys. The only time I drove the car these days was when I took her for a walk along the river. She hobbled to the door and wiggled her arse about. I took Jim by the arm and walked him out to the car, which was sitting in the driveway waiting for us, its roof covered in a blanket of fallen leaves. I opened the passenger door, helped Jim into the seat and buckled him in. Ella had run out of the house and hurled herself in after him before I could stop her. She worked her body between the front bucket seats onto the back seat. Before I could close the door again, the cat had leapt up from the driveway onto Jim's lap.

'Good girl,' he whispered. 'Good girl.'

I reached into the car and grabbed the cat by the neck, ready to throw it out.

'It will have to stay here, Jim.'

He pulled the cat protectively to his chest.

'No, she won't. Come on, Matthew. Jump in. She'll do just nice with me.'

'Jim …'

'I said, she'll be right with me,' he ordered, as forcefully as he could.

It was raining and I was getting soaked. Jim turned his head away from me and caressed the cat behind its ears. I gave in to his demand, ran around to the other side of the car and jumped in.

'This is getting heavier, Jim. Keep your window wound up or we'll cop a pelting.'

I turned on the ignition and the wipers. He knocked at the side door.

'This is a German car.'

'Yep. It is.'

'We'll be right then. The Germans would have won the war if they'd stuck to engineering instead of trying to knock the whole world off.'

'Really?'

'Absolutely.'

I pulled out of the drive, switched on the headlights and drove up the road.

'Did you fight in the war, Jim? You've never mentioned it.'

'Not me. I was too young. Good luck, that. But I made money out of it, when it was over. Importing salvaged army gear, reconditioning it and selling it on. Up the bush, mostly.'

He stuck his nose against the side window and looked out into the night, to the lights of the city in the distance. He held up the sleeve of his dressing gown and inspected the pattern of lilac hibiscus flowers. This disturbed the cat, and it wasn't happy. It jumped from his lap into mine – and dug its claws into my crotch.

I screamed in pain. Jim jumped in his seat.

'Where are we heading, Matthew? Where you bloody taking me?' He suddenly sounded lost and confused.

I held one hand on the steering wheel as I tried extracting the cat and calming Jim at the same time. It had got between my legs, wrapped itself around a thigh and stabbed its claws deeper into me.

I reached down and grabbed it by the neck.

Jim was almost crying, 'Where are we going?'

'For ice-cream, Jim,' I yelled. 'You wanted chocolate fucking ice-cream.'

He leaned across the car and stared down at the cat.

'Hey, watch what you're doing there. You'll hurt—' he looked up, 'watch out, son. Look out!'

We were hurtling downhill, towards a hairpin turn in the road. The river lay straight ahead.

I let go of the cat, gripped the steering wheel with both hands and slammed on the brakes.

'Hold on, Jim. *Hold on.*'

The car shuddered as the tyres tried gripping the wet road – we smashed through a hedge. It was all that had separated us from the river. The VW left the road and momentarily glided through the night sky. I turned my head away and saw Jim's eyes light up.

He pointed to the city skyline. 'Hey, look at that. It's real pretty.'

Then we crashed into the water.

The car jarred violently from side to side and I felt Ella's body slam against the back of my seat. She landed on the floor, jammed between the front and back seats.

I unbuckled my seatbelt, turned and rested a hand on her back.

'It's all right, old girl. It's all right.'

She looked up and licked the back of my hand as I patted her.

The cat had somehow found its way back onto Jim's lap. Its fur was standing on end.

Jim stared out of the front windscreen as he nursed her. He didn't look hurt and seemed calm. The car bobbed gently up and down in the water.

I switched the wipers to full speed and peered through the windscreen. 'Can you swim, Jim?'

He thought about the question for a moment.

'That's a hard one. I couldn't really say. But we'll find out quick if she starts sinking.'

He looked down at his feet.

'We're pretty high and dry at the minute. Good car, this one. Does she belong to you?'

'Well, not technically. The car's still in my wife's name.'

'She won't be too happy then?'

'Who knows. It wasn't worth much.'

The car began to sink and we were taking on water. It rocked from side to side in the current and then stopped moving. I unwound the window. We were not far off the bank. I opened my door and stuck one leg out of the car. We were resting in around a metre of water.

'Hey, Jim. We're okay. It's not too deep.'

He patted me on the shoulder.

'Well manoeuvred, son. Good work.'

Ella always loved a swim. I encouraged her into the water. She paddled to the bank and sat watching the car with curiosity. I helped Jim out of the car, nursing the cat in my arms.

'Can you walk to the bank? Maybe I should piggy-back you?'

He was shivering with the cold and was turning blue.

'Good as gold,' he chattered through his false teeth.

We began walking up the hill back to our street. The cold wind cut through my dressing gown and my wet feet had turned to ice. A car travelling in the opposite direction flashed its lights, did a U-turn and pulled into the kerb. It was another neighbour, Ethan Morris, the son of a doctor who lived two doors down from me. He wound down the window of an old Toyota he was driving, a vehicle in a worse state than mine.

'You two want a lift home?'

I tried to answer but couldn't get my frostbitten jaw unlocked. I nodded my head as best I could, opened the back door, helped Jim and the cat into a seat, followed by Ella. I jumped in the front seat. The car reeked of marijuana smoke. Ethan turned to Jim and Ella and then me, glassy-eyed.

'What have you four been doing?' he drawled.

I still couldn't open my mouth. I was glad in a way, as I didn't know what to say.

'Ice-cream,' Jim explained. 'We have been out getting some ice-cream. I think we've got it here somewhere.'

'Cool,' the kid nodded. 'I love my ice-cream.'

ACKNOWLEDGMENTS

I want to thank John Hunter for his unwavering support of my writing. I also want to thank everyone at UQP associated with the delivery of this book – a dedicated team effort.

I am fortunate to have a wonderfully supportive family and a group of loyal friends. This is for you. For Sara – 'We're riding out tonight to case the Promised Land'. And finally, Tully (1999–2013) – we miss your mighty big heart.